You're About to Become a
Privileged Woman.

INTRODUCING
PAGES & PRIVILEGES™.

It's our way of thanking you for buying
our books at your favorite retail store.

GET ALL THIS FREE
WITH JUST ONE PROOF OF PURCHASE:

◆ Hotel Discounts up to 60% at home and abroad

◆ Travel Service - Guaranteed lowest published
airfares plus 5% cash back on tickets

◆ $25 Travel Voucher

◆ Sensuous Petite Parfumerie collection ($50 value)

◆ Insider Tips Letter with sneak previews of
upcoming books

◆ Mystery Gift (if you enroll before 6/15/95)

You'll get a F
It's your passport
even more grea

There's no club to join. No

D1040528

n.

As a *Privileged Woman,* you'll be entitled to all these *Free Benefits.* And *Free Gifts,* too.

To thank you for buying our books, we've designed an exclusive FREE program called *PAGES & PRIVILEGES™*. You can enroll with just one Proof of Purchase, and get the kind of luxuries that, until now, you could only read about.

*B*IG HOTEL DISCOUNTS

A privileged woman stays in the finest hotels. And so can you—at up to 60% off! Imagine standing in a hotel check-in line and watching as the guest in front of you pays $150 for the same room that's only costing you $60. Your *Pages & Privileges* discounts are good at Sheraton, Marriott, Best Western, Hyatt and thousands of other fine hotels all over the U.S., Canada and Europe.

*F*REE DISCOUNT TRAVEL SERVICE

A privileged woman is always jetting to romantic places. When <u>you</u> fly, just make one phone call for the lowest published airfare at time of booking—<u>or double the difference back!</u> PLUS—

you'll get a $25 voucher to use the first time you book a flight AND <u>5% cash back on every ticket you buy thereafter through the travel service!</u>

*F*REE GIFTS!

A privileged woman is always getting wonderful gifts.
Luxuriate in rich fragrances that will stir your senses (and his). This gift-boxed assortment of fine perfumes includes three popular scents, each in a beautiful designer bottle.  Truly Lace...This luxurious fragrance unveils your sensuous side. L'Effleur...discover the romance of the Victorian era with this soft floral. Muguet des bois...a single note floral of singular beauty. This $50 value is yours—FREE when you enroll in *Pages & Privileges*! And it's just the beginning of the gifts and benefits that will be coming your way!

*F*REE INSIDER TIPS LETTER

A privileged woman is always informed. And you'll be, too, with our free letter full of fascinating information and sneak previews of upcoming books.

*M*ORE GREAT GIFTS & BENEFITS TO COME

A privileged woman always has a lot to look forward to.
And so will you. You get all these wonderful FREE gifts and benefits now with only one purchase...and there are no additional purchases required. However, each additional retail purchase of Harlequin and Silhouette books brings you a step closer to even more great FREE benefits like half-price movie tickets...and even more FREE gifts like these beautiful fragrance gift baskets:

L'Effleur...This basketful of romance lets you discover L'Effleur from head to toe, heart to home.

Truly Lace...A basket spun with the sensuous luxuries of Truly Lace, including Dusting Powder in a reusable satin and lace covered box.

*E*NROLL *N*OW!
Complete the Enrollment Form on the back of this card and become a Privileged Woman today!

Enroll Today in *PAGES & PRIVILEGES*™, the program that gives you Great Gifts and Benefits with just one purchase!

Enrollment Form

☐ *Yes!* I WANT TO BE A *PRIVILEGED WOMAN.*
　　Enclosed is one *PAGES & PRIVILEGES*™ Proof of Purchase from any Harlequin or Silhouette book currently for sale in stores (Proofs of Purchase are found on the back pages of books) and the store cash register receipt. Please enroll me in *PAGES & PRIVILEGES*™. Send my Welcome Kit and FREE Gifts -- and activate my FREE benefits -- immediately.

NAME (please print)

ADDRESS　　　　　　　　　　　　　　　　　　　　　**APT. NO**

CITY　　　　　**STATE**　　　　　**ZIP/POSTAL CODE**

► DETACH HERE AND MAIL TODAY! ►

PROOF OF PURCHASE

SAMPLE ONLY

Please allow 6-8 weeks for delivery. Quantities are limited. We reserve the right to substitute items. Enroll before October 31, 1995 and receive one full year of benefits.

NO CLUB!
NO COMMITMENT!
Just one purchase brings you great Free Gifts and Benefits!
(See inside for details.)

Name of store where this book was purchased_____

Date of purchase_____

Type of store:

　☐ Bookstore　☐ Supermarket　☐ Drugstore

　☐ Dept. or discount store (e.g. K-Mart or Walmart)

　☐ Other (specify)_____

Which Harlequin or Silhouette series do you usually read?

_____

Complete and mail with one Proof of Purchase and store receipt to:

U.S.: *PAGES & PRIVILEGES*™, P.O. Box 1960, Danbury, CT 06813-1960

Canada: *PAGES & PRIVILEGES*™, 49-6A The Donway West, P.O. 813, North York, ON M3C 2E8　　　　PRINTED IN U.S.A

"*I wanted to tell you certain things.*"

Damien smiled encouragement, confident of holding his influence over Natalie's thoughts and actions. "Go ahead and tell me," he invited, gesturing with open hands.

"For one thing, I don't want you guarding me like a watchdog, anymore."

His smile turned rueful. "It was only for your own protection, Natalie. You were... rather lost and defenseless."

"Well, I've found my defenses again."

"Fine!"

EMMA DARCY nearly became an actress until her fiancé declared he preferred to attend the theater with her. She became a wife and mother. Later, she took up oil painting—unsuccessfully, she remarks. Then she tried architecture, designing the family home in New South Wales. Next came romance writing—"the hardest and most challenging of all the activities," she confesses.

Books by Emma Darcy

HARLEQUIN PRESENTS
1536—AN IMPOSSIBLE DREAM
1632—THE SHINING OF LOVE
1659—A WEDDING TO REMEMBER
1679—IN NEED OF A WIFE
1721—BURNING WITH PASSION

Don't miss any of our special offers. Write to us at the following address for information on our newest releases.

Harlequin Reader Service
U.S.: 3010 Walden Ave., P.O. Box 1325, Buffalo, NY 14269
Canadian: P.O. Box 609, Fort Erie, Ont. L2A 5X3

EMMA DARCY

The Fatherhood Affair

Harlequin Books

TORONTO • NEW YORK • LONDON
AMSTERDAM • PARIS • SYDNEY • HAMBURG
STOCKHOLM • ATHENS • TOKYO • MILAN
MADRID • WARSAW • BUDAPEST • AUCKLAND

ISBN 0-373-11745-0

THE FATHERHOOD AFFAIR

Copyright © 1995 by Emma Darcy.

First North American Publication 1995.

CHAPTER ONE

A GREAT deal could be done in two months.

The thought brought a feeling of satisfaction to Natalie Hayes as she walked from the foyer of the Regent Hotel and up the grand staircase leading to Kable's Restaurant. Today she intended to show Damien Chandler precisely how much could be done in two months, and how much could be made to happen.

This luncheon was the ideal occasion to let Damien know she didn't need him as a watchdog any more. She could take care of herself. Damien's sense of duty—or was it guilt?—could finally be laid to rest.

She was back to her best weight. The bold orange dress was light-years away from any suggestion of lingering bereavement. It hugged her curves and highlighted both her recently acquired tan and the artful blonde streaks in her radically restyled hair. Damien couldn't call her a pale ghost of herself today.

Her face had colour. She no longer had hollows in her cheeks. She had played up her light amber eyes with a subtle shading of brown and gold. The shorter, softer, brighter hairstyle suited her face much better than the long and rather lifeless

5

fall of honey-coloured hair she had simply let grow in the past twelve months. Natalie was satisfied she looked quite pretty again, younger, and certainly up-to-date in every fashion sense.

She had felt absolutely confident about walking into this hotel, one of the classiest hotels in Sydney. She looked like a new woman. She felt like a new woman. She *was* a new woman.

There was a buoyant lilt of anticipation in her step as she reached the landing that led to the highly reputed restaurant. She was going to enjoy the surprise in Damien's eyes. He would have to realise, must be made to realise, that she no longer required a crutch or a spur or advice or criticism. All these things he had supplied in abundance over the past year. It was time to bring it to a halt. A dead halt.

She saw him seated on the sofa beyond the receptionist's desk. He was hunched forward, apparently contemplating the drink in his hand. Despite an air of weariness, probably from jet lag, he looked as impressive as he always did. A three-piece grey suit had the expensive sheen of silk in the fabric. Tailored for him in Hong Kong, Natalie surmised.

He glanced up and saw her.

The shock of recognition on his face was not the reaction Natalie had expected. Surprise, yes. She had hoped to surprise him. She had not expected a reaction that arrested all movement, dulled even further the light in his eyes, an outright withdrawal away from her into himself.

It was too extreme for Damien. It mangled the smile that had been hovering inside her. It sent an odd tingle of apprehension down her spine. She stopped walking. She was assailed by the sense of having a comfortable familiarity forcibly taken away from her.

Natalie had never seen Damien Chandler completely thrown by anything. He was always in charge of himself. He was always in charge of everything and everyone within his ambit. It was nigh on impossible to tell what went on inside the man. He revealed that to no one.

In the space of a few seconds, she saw total shock, followed by a twist of anguish, a jaw-clenching look of determination, veiled anger, then a plainly visible relaxation of his features into a smile of forced, lukewarm pleasure as he put his glass down and rose to his feet.

'Natalie...' He managed to inject both surprise and delight into his voice, although what he really felt Natalie had no idea. He moved to meet her. 'What a joy to see you looking so brilliantly alive!'

Damien was a master of such blandishments. Natalie had heard him do it to every woman he had met over the years they had known each other. It sounded right. It was what she had wanted to hear. But something was missing. That *something* was approval. She couldn't see it in his eyes.

Not that she needed Damien's approval. It was simply that...why were his eyes full of questions instead of recognising she had answered all the criticisms he had angrily impressed on her at their last meeting?

Then he took hold of her hands as though it was the most natural thing in the world to do. But it wasn't. Not with her. She had seen him perform the same welcoming gesture with other women, making a flirtatious intimacy of it and often accompanying it with a light kiss. He had never tried it with her. Never! Not even when she was Brett's bride and Damien was best man at their wedding.

Her shoulder muscles stiffened as electric prickles ran up her arm. She didn't understand what was going on. Damien wasn't supposed to step out of the mould he had established in her mind as Brett's closest friend and business partner. She did want him to drop the role of self-appointed guardian to Brett's widow, but...his uncharacteristic behaviour was ruining everything.

It was a relief that he didn't try to press any closer. If he had, she would have recoiled, unable to prevent the reflex action. As it was, she was acutely aware of the warmth and strength of the fingers enclosing hers, and the caressing graze of his thumbs across her knuckles.

'I leave you a pale shadow of yourself, and I come back to find you glowing,' he said in light bemusement, his tone belying the intense probe of his eyes. 'You benefit from my absence. Is there some special reason behind the change?'

Natalie shrugged. 'Lots of reasons.' He was one of them. She forced a smile. 'Wasn't it your intention to jolt me into getting on with my life?'

'The result is stunning.'

'But you don't like it.'

'I prefer to have more time in which to make a judgement.'

He looked at her in a way he had never overtly looked at her before. Raw, jungle hunger. Natalie was stunned by the sudden blaze of uncloaked desire in his eyes. It burnt into her, making her feel naked and exposed. It bore no relation whatsoever to the kind and supportive business friendship they were supposed to be having. It sizzled with unrepressed sexuality.

She felt her heart catch. Her mind jumbled chaotically around the thought that Damien now saw her as different from the unexciting *hausfrau* she had been. And he was letting her *know* it. Without hesitation, he was jettisoning all of their past. The years of keeping his distance from her had just winked out.

He meant to have her. No doubt about that. Knowing Damien as she did, Natalie realised she would have her hands full trying to stop him. The charge of animal electricity coming from him had her nerves leaping like fire-crackers.

He released her hands. Natalie's relief was short-lived. He smoothly moved to link one of her arms around his for escorting her into the restaurant. His eyes didn't leave hers. 'Hungry?' he asked.

She wondered what type of hunger he had on his mind. 'Yes,' she said lightly, trying to fight the unsettling effect of his closeness.

Taking her arm was an ordinary enough courtesy. It was absurd to have this skittish feeling of wanting to shy away from him, to put more distance between them. He couldn't seduce *her* into taking him as a lover. It would be like involving herself with Brett all over again. She wouldn't consider it. Not in a million years. Damien had better put it out of his mind or this luncheon would come to a very abrupt end.

He gestured their readiness to the *maître d'*, who smiled and set off to lead them to their table.

Natalie registered that the smile was a typical female response to Damien. Most women would classify him as outstanding in the tall, dark and handsome category. Add to that the charisma of keen intelligence, a charm of manner based on rock-solid self-assurance, and the attention he drew was perfectly reasonable.

As they passed tables where women were seated, interested looks were cast his way. Damien Chandler commanded a second glance from everyone, men included. He carried the air of being *someone*. He stood out from the general run. People noticed him, remembered him. Such attributes were both social and business assets. Objectively, Natalie had recognised this long ago.

She would never have believed that the simple act of having her arm linked to his would make anything different, but it did. The looks directed at Damien slid to her, looks of envy and assessment, matching her against him as a couple. It did nothing for Natalie's self-confidence.

All the same, Damien was not going to sweep her off her feet. She didn't care how many women fancied him or how fanciable he was. She knew better than to lay her head on his chopping-block. Easy come, easy go. She had seen it too many times to be even faintly interested. That he could be turned on by her new image was virtually an insulting demonstration of how facile his sexual urges were.

Damien would never marry. Of that she felt certain. He had done it once, in his mid-twenties before they had ever met. From all accounts, it had been his wife who had walked out on him. Which carried its own message to Natalie.

She was glad to reach their table and be seated. She concentrated on laying her shoulder-bag beside the leg of her chair, smiling at the hovering waiter, ordering a champagne cocktail, smoothing the table napkin across her lap. The actions gave her time to recover some of the sense of well-being and purpose with which she had started out for this meeting.

She felt Damien's gaze on her and glanced up to meet it, determined on acting naturally. 'How was your trip?' she asked.

'Successful.'

That was normal. Damien was a powerhouse of energy and inspiration. She smiled. 'Does this mean you'll be back and forth to Hong Kong for the foreseeable future?'

'No.'

His thick black lashes swept down. Combined with deeply set eyelids, they had the effect of making his eyes look dark from a distance. Their silvery-grey colour came as an intriguing surprise. When he looked up his expression was flintlike and purposeful.

'I've sold the company, Natalie. It's being taken over by a Chinese consortium that wants to spread its interests out of Hong Kong. If it's allowed to do so.'

She was dumbstruck. Changes were coming thick and fast today. She could hardly put two thoughts together. Concern for him slashed through her mind, prompting the question, 'Were you in financial trouble, Damien? Did paying me Brett's share . . .'

'No,' he answered curtly. 'As I told you before, and as cruel as it may seem, Brett's death . . .' He didn't go on.

' . . . was my financial solution,' she concluded for him. The solution to several other problems as well, she thought bitterly. But the cost of it was still difficult to bear.

'I never wish to refer to the matter again,' Damien said, a hostility in his voice.

'You're not selling the company because of me,' Natalie protested. 'You can have the money back if you need it. I haven't touched it.'

'It has nothing to do with money, Natalie. I simply want to be out.'

'Why? You're so good at what you do. Surely...' Her mind clicked on to another path. Was it because Brett was gone? Damien was superb at selling conversions for computer programs. He was brilliant at working out what was required by the clients, but Brett had been the force behind delivering what was promised. His was the genius that had put it all together and made it work.

'It's not the same without Brett,' Damien said flatly. 'The company has the personnel and expertise to carry on. It's still a viable business, Natalie. But I miss Brett's quick understanding of what's needed. I'm reminded of him all the time. It was something we shared.'

'Yes. Yes, I know.'

They'd been as close as, if not closer than brothers. That wasn't to say they never fought over issues. They did. Like cats and dogs. In the end, they always stood together, no matter what.

Their loyalty to each other was so strong that it overrode the loyalty owed to her.

The waiter brought their drinks and handed them menus. Natalie stared blindly at the printed list for several moments, realising for the first time that Damien's grief had probably been as deep as her own. Worse, in the sense that he had been abseiling on the cliff, a helpless witness as first Ryan, then Brett, trying to save their son, fell to their deaths. At least she had been spared that.

Natalie fought back tears. She had to put her dead child behind her. She had to put the misery behind her. She had let grief swallow up her life long enough. She was not going to let her resolution slip now. She selected the Caesar salad as an entrée, and the Atlantic salmon for her main course, then set the menu aside.

Damien was watching her.

She raised her eyebrows. 'So what do you plan to do?'

He relaxed. 'I'm obliged to stay on with the company for six months to ease the change-over. There's a three-year exclusion clause from taking on any similar type of work.'

'That's quite a lot of time to fill in.'

'I have a project in mind.'

'What is it?'

He looked intently at her, as though there should be some intimate understanding between them. 'Don't you have any idea?'

'None whatsoever,' she answered airily.

'That makes everything a little more difficult.'

He paused a minute, reassessing the situation. She gave him no encouragement. She kept an expression of bland curiosity pasted on her face.

'What are your plans, Natalie?' he asked, deciding to approach his purpose from another angle. 'Did you come to this meeting with a definite idea as to its outcome?'

An appalling thought struck her. Had Damien interpreted her new image as an attempt to attract him? Natalie burned with embarrassment. How could he entertain such an implausible idea? Perhaps, though, that was why he had looked at her in the way he did. The need to rectify any misunderstanding caused her amber eyes to glitter with fiery golden sparks.

'Yes, I did.'

'Well?'

'I wanted to tell you certain things.'

He smiled encouragement, confident of holding his influence over her thoughts and actions. 'Go ahead and tell me,' he invited, gesturing with open hands.

'For one thing, I don't want you guarding me like a watchdog any more.'

His smile turned rueful. 'It was only for your protection, Natalie. You were . . . rather lost and defenceless.'

'Well, I've found my defences again.'

'Fine!'

'And I never want to hear another word of criticism from you. It's my life and I'll live it as I see fit. Not as you see fit.'

That sobered him. His eyes went still and wary.

Her chin lifted in defiant self determination. 'I don't want you to ever mention Brett again in my hearing,' she added strongly. Her flow of thought then faltered under his hard, relentless stare.

'Is that all?' he asked tersely.

'More or less,' she answered. 'But I'll think of more if you press me.'

'In other words, you want *me* out of your life.'

'Yes.'

'As a business advisor and as a friend?'

'Yes.'

He left her no alternative if he wanted to mix sex with friendship. Her gratitude for what he *had* done for her didn't extend that far. Nevertheless, she did feel a certain hollowness burrowing through her stomach. He had been like a cog around which her life had turned for a long time. A mainstay. Her head swam a little with the enormity of cutting free from him. Did she really want that?

'Is there another man?' His harsh tone of voice verged on the critical.

Natalie's eyes flared. 'Not yet. But there will be.'

He returned a steely challenge. 'What do you really want, Natalie?'

Had he somehow read her mind? Sensed the doubt? The fearful uncertainty in severing all ties? Natalie focused hard on the question. If she was going to be her own woman, she had to know the answer. It came to her in a burst of bright clarity.

'The best thing that ever happened to me was Ryan. I can't replace him. He was a unique and wonderful child. But I can have another child who can be just as unique and wonderful, Damien. That's what I intend to have.'

Damien sat back abruptly in his chair. Once again his face reflected shock. He stared at her as though he had never known her, an unseeing blankness in his eyes, all the clever intelligence frozen, or turned inward.

It sent a chill through Natalie's heart. He had left her. The impulse to draw him back surged through her so wildly, words were spilling off her tongue before she could stop them.

'Aren't you glad to be rid of me? Aren't you glad to have any responsibility to me set aside?'

The taunt succeeded. His eyes refocused on hers. 'No.'

The stark negative gave her nothing to work on. Damn the man and his self-sufficiency! Why couldn't he reveal what was going on inside him?

'What purpose is there in our ever seeing each other again?' she pressed. 'Give me one good reason.'

'Your husband was my friend,' he said slowly, picking his words with care. 'However much you think he loved you, I believe he was no friend to you.'

The import of those words was not lost on Natalie. She sat very still, holding her breath. Damien's loyalty to Brett was cracking. Would he now speak the truth about her husband, reveal the infidelities he had helped to cover up? Did Damien even suspect how much she already knew, or was he still convinced he and Brett had artfully concealed everything?

He leaned forward. As though he had flicked a switch that flung open the windows of his mind, his eyes once more blazed with naked desire.

'The reason I sold the company was to have the time to prove to you—conclusively and forever—that you married the wrong man, Natalie.' The low throb of passion in his voice gathered a deep soul-shaking conviction as he added, 'The man you should have married was me. Not Brett. *Me*!'

CHAPTER TWO

MARRIAGE? To Damien?

Natalie felt as though she had been pummelled in the solar plexus. Her mind was blown into whirling confusion. She stared incredulously at Damien, struggling to connect what she knew of him to the words he had spoken. He held her gaze, relentlessly reinforcing what he'd said with compelling intensity.

She supposed she should feel flattered... a man of his many attractions wanting *her*. She wondered what influenced his choice. He hadn't mentioned love. She wasn't the first woman he'd wanted, and wouldn't be the last. So why her?

Natalie's shell-shocked mind finally grasped the motive behind Damien's statement.

Brett.

She felt sick.

And angry.

She leaned forward, her eyes a golden shower of blistering sparks. 'Even now, with Brett in the grave, you can't help competing with him, can you? You can't let go. You want to take me over to prove to your insatiable ego that you were the better man.'

He grimaced in frustration. 'That's nonsense! Why are you avoiding the obvious?'

'The obvious is that Brett's still on your mind,' she retorted. 'You began and ended your ridiculous claim with Brett. After I'd specifically asked you never to mention him to me again.'

'So it still hurts that much, does it? Goddammit, Natalie, I've waited long enough! Will you recognise me for what I am?'

'That's the problem, Damien. I do recognise you for what you are. You told me straight out that you sold the company because it wasn't any fun without Brett. It was something you *shared*. So what's the new project? *Me*. Something else you can share with him in some tormented, twisted, perverted way.'

'I'm not sharing you with anyone,' he declared indignantly. 'When I saw you today...'

'You thought the *fun* could begin.'

From somewhere inside her came a billow of outrage. It activated a burst of adrenalin. She reached down, snatched her shoulder-bag from the floor, opened it, and grabbed her wallet.

'I thought you had finally put your grief behind you,' Damien continued.

'I will not be beholden to you for anything, Damien.' She found a twenty-dollar note and slapped it on the table. 'That will pay for our drinks. I don't want to eat with you. I don't want to be with you. I will never, in any circumstance, *sleep* with you. Do you understand what those words mean?'

'So the brave new front is just a charade,' he mocked angrily. 'You can't face up to a different reality.'

'What's different?' She returned her wallet to her bag and stood up, casting him a look of contempt. 'If you want to prove you're a better man than Brett, you can run after all the women he had on the side.'

'What?' He looked astounded, incredulous. 'You knew?'

'Of course I knew. And your part in it, as well.'

'I played no part in it . . .'

'Don't lie to me, Damien. You covered up for Brett. He deceived me. You betrayed me.'

Disdaining to glance at Damien again, Natalie set off down the length of the dining-room to the exit of the restaurant.

'Natalie . . .' It was both a protest and an appeal.

She ignored it. She heard Damien coming after her, brushing past hovering waiters, but she neither turned her head nor slowed her pace. She felt utterly deflated and cast down. She should never have trusted the feeling that he meant well by her. It was a sham so he could win out in the end. Against a dead man.

As she stepped into the reception nook outside the restaurant, Damien caught her arm, forcibly halting her. She gave him an intimidating stare of icy rejection.

'What did you want from me that I didn't give?' he demanded. 'Tell me one thing.'

'Approval. As in a-p-p-r-o-v-a-l. APPROVAL as in block letters. *Approval* as in italics. Simply approval. That's what I wanted from you, Damien. That's what you never gave me. Not even today.'

'You've always had that, Natalie.'

'Never.'

He dragged in a deep breath. 'I'm sorry I was impatient with your grieving for Brett. Terribly sorry.'

'I was grieving for Ryan, not Brett. Brett had whittled away my love for him. There was none left.'

'How was I to know that? You never gave any indication. I never realised you were disillusioned with your marriage.'

'Who parades private pain in public?'

His eyes narrowed. 'How would you have reacted if I'd come running to tell you about Brett's affairs? You would have hated me for it, Natalie.'

'It would have destroyed your friendship,' she mocked.

She wrenched her arm out of his grasp and headed for the staircase. What he said hurt. It bit painfully into her psyche. The deep-seated sense of rejection, the sense of failure, of being a discard, inadequate.

Damien fell into step beside her. 'What makes you think I covered up for him?'

'I know.'

'Give me one example.'

'You slipped up at the funeral.' She paused at the head of the stairs to face him with bleak derisive eyes. 'The woman who went on the camp with you and Brett that weekend...it was reported that she was your companion, Damien. She wasn't.'

'She was,' he insisted.

'Don't think I'm ungrateful for your discretion. If the media had latched on to the fact that adultery was mixed up with the death of my son and my husband, they would have had more of a field day than they did.'

'Natalie, I swear before God she was with *me*. I invited her. I took her there. She shared my tent. Brett had Ryan with him.'

She shook her head. 'It doesn't add up, Damien. She wept copiously at the funeral. You didn't go near her. Not one word or gesture of comfort.'

'I didn't leave *your* side,' he asserted with passion. 'She meant nothing to me. She was keen on abseiling. I asked her on the trip to make it a foursome instead of a threesome. I wasn't to know you were going to be too sick to come. We were already there at the campsite when Brett arrived without you.'

Was he speaking the truth? Had she misread the situation? 'How did Ryan get so close to the edge of the cliff? Why wasn't Brett watching him? Ryan was a sensible little boy. He would have obeyed his father.'

'Natalie, for God's sake! Accidents can happen so quickly. Don't torture yourself like this.'

'It doesn't matter any more,' she said dully. 'Nothing can bring my beautiful little boy back.'

She started down the staircase. She had to get away from all this. It wasn't doing her any good, raking over the miseries of the past. She had to look to the future, break with Damien now, start a new life. That was abundantly clear.

Damien wasn't a friend. And that hurt, too. In his way, he had acted honourably towards her. Yet she had known he had the same attitude towards challenges as Brett had. They were two of a kind. She simply hadn't anticipated that he would see *her* as a challenge.

He was matching steps with her, still not prepared to let her walk away from him. 'Why didn't you leave Brett?' he asked.

She didn't answer. She couldn't imagine any man would understand. Trapped by a pregnancy...making excuses. Trapped by wanting the best for her baby...making compromises. Hoping things would change. Wanting to believe in renewed promises because the sense of failure was too hard to face.

Brett wasn't all bad. Mostly, but not all. She had fallen in love with his joy in living, his wit, his charm, his exuberant personality, the athletic body he made master of any physical challenge, the mind that thrived on solving problems few others could. She had thought herself the luckiest woman in the world that Brett Hayes had fallen in love with her.

She had never considered herself anyone special. She was averagely pretty, helped along by a better than average figure that had been very firm and trim when she had met Brett. She had been working then as a bush-walking guide, supplementing an irregular income from the paintings she sold to the tourists who flocked to her hometown. Noosa was a very popular seaside resort on the Sunshine Coast of Queensland, and Brett had been one more tourist, indulging his love of the outdoors, and sweeping Natalie into a marriage that had seemed idyllic. At first.

She had come to realise, painfully, that Brett saw women as a challenge, too. All of them. He couldn't resist testing himself, over and over again. Natalie he had put in a completely separate category. She was his chosen wife. The mother of his child.

Ryan . . . always Ryan stopping her from taking that final step away from Brett. He was indisputably a loving father, proud of his son. Ryan had adored his Daddy. She simply hadn't been able to bring herself to deprive them of the relationship that was naturally theirs. In the end, it would have saved Ryan's life—both their lives—if she had. She shook off the torment of 'if only's.

'Brett felt inadequate,' Damien declared. 'He...'

'Don't be absurd,' Natalie answered coldly.

Brett was the most gifted, talented individual she had met in her life. A bright golden god among other men. *Brett made other people feel inadequate*. People like Damien. People like herself.

Damien touched her arm to try to draw her attention back to him. 'If you knew about his infidelities, why didn't you divorce him? What stopped you?' he asked, exasperation creeping into his voice.

They had reached the foyer. It didn't really matter what she said to Damien. Whether he comprehended it or not was irrelevant. She was not going to see him again. She glanced at him with determined finality and gave him the one reason that had kept her with Brett.

'He was the father of my child.'

She didn't pause to gauge his reaction to that bare statement. She had no intention of explaining or embellishing it. She took a direct line towards the doors that led out of the hotel. This meeting with Damien had been a disaster from start to finish. She was ashamed of having been deluded into thinking he actually cared about her as a person.

Of course, she had realised that to Damien she was an extension of Brett, but there had been thoughtful gestures from him which she had believed were for her sake alone. She had thought he cared about her interests, suggesting ways of developing and extending her creative talent. She had no idea he was so...well, almost deranged...in his obsession about Brett.

Tears blurred her eyes. She had looked forward to telling Damien about the commission to illustrate a children's book. Damien had taught her creative graphic design. She had imagined him being pleased for her. She had actively gone after the job and got it, an achievement she was sure would earn his approval. Finally.

She had tried so hard to get her life moving again in order to please him. She was proud of her efforts over the past two months. She had wanted Damien to be *proud* of her.

Disappointment wrenched her heart. This was her second bad mistake, letting another man like Brett get close to her. At least Damien wasn't pressing any more questions on her. She was grateful for his silence as he accompanied her out to the covered driveway that serviced the hotel. As far as she was concerned, there was nothing more to say. Except goodbye. Forever.

'Taxi?' the doorman asked.

'Please,' Natalie answered.

'We need to talk this through, Natalie,' Damien murmured as the doorman moved forward to summon the first cab from the rank in the street below.

'No point,' she demurred.

'You have some serious misconceptions...'

'Mine have already been sorted out. Yours haven't.'

'Look at me!' he commanded in exasperation.

'I don't want to.'

She kept her gaze steadfastly locked on the taxi turning slowly up the duel driveway, taking the lane closest to the hotel entrance. She couldn't bear to see that blaze of desire in Damien's eyes again. It reduced her to nothing but another potential conquest.

'I've a lot to say to you,' he burst out.

'I've heard enough.'

'You can't dismiss five years in five minutes and reduce it to nothing, Natalie.'

'Watch me.'

'Give me the chance to explain. You owe me that.'

'I didn't ask you for anything, Damien. You gave it.'

'You accepted it.'

'Call me stupid. I didn't understand what my role was,' she said bitterly. 'I didn't realise I was supposed to become another bed partner.'

'You're the woman I want in my life.'

'For the present.'

'Give it a chance.'

'So you can play and lay while I have your children?' She turned derisive eyes to his as the taxi halted in front of her. 'No, thanks, Damien. I've been through that once. Perhaps the next woman you feed that line to will be more accommodating. Goodbye and good luck to you.'

The passenger door of the taxi was held open for her by the hotel employee. She stepped forward and swung herself into the back seat.

'Natalie...'

She ignored the urgency in Damien's voice, but she couldn't ignore the strong bulk of his body.

'I'm coming with you.' His powerfully muscled thigh pressed against hers.

She hastily scrambled to the other side of the seat. 'No, you're not,' she protested.

'Otherwise we will never see each other again.'

'That's what I want.'

He closed the door. The inside of the car suddenly seemed filled with his presence. It pulsed with an energy that clutched at her heart and caused her senses to sharpen alarmingly.

'It's over!' she cried, feverishly desperate in her need to convince him.

'It never started,' he replied, a rough edge of passion in his voice.

'It wasn't meant to be.'

He turned to her, his face stripped of any civilised veneer. Raw, jungle hunger leapt from his eyes and impaled her.

'I won't accept you judging me by your experience with Brett.'

Her mind swam with the realisation that she had underestimated Damien. She shouldn't have likened him to Brett. He was as dark in nature as Brett was bright. Dark and deep and intense, and with all his unleashed energy, indefinably dangerous.

For years she had wondered what went on inside him. What restraints he had...and, if all his secret longings were bared, what would a woman experience? The thought had intrigued her. She was getting more than a glimpse of the answer now, and it both fascinated and frightened her. She saw a primitive male hunter, relentless in his determination to track down his quarry, unstoppable.

She shivered. 'I don't want you, Damien. I don't want you.' She heard the wary, almost excited note in her voice, and didn't care as long as he got the message.

'What would happen if I took you in my arms, Natalie?' His eyes burned down to the agitated rise and fall of her breasts as she took quick breaths to calm her pulse-rate. 'If I were to kiss and caress you...'

'Stop it! I won't listen! Go away!'

But the images evoked did have an insidiously seductive power. Damien might be the hunter, but as a woman she knew if she tossed over the traces, threw everything upon the wind... anything and everything was possible. There had been solitary, vulnerable moments when she had fantasised ... Damien wild, irrepressible, adoring her, approving of her, being proud of her. They had been some kind of solace at the time when Brett was entertaining himself with some other woman.

She had sternly repressed such wicked thoughts. That they should focus on her husband's best friend made them even more reprehensible. They were not fitting for a married woman who considered herself moral and decent. It dragged her down to Brett's level. Natalie had been ashamed of herself that they had occurred at all.

Now Damien wanted to do what she had forbidden herself to think about. More. Natalie felt there was some key to her mind and heart and body, and if some man was to unlatch the lock... Brett had had the key for a while but he had thrown it away.

Damien probably had the key, too, but it would not last. The experience would be wild and wonderful and dangerous, and in the end, as with Brett, would cost her too much. She had to stop this now, not let Damien tempt her into something she knew would lead to more hurt and disillusionment. Men didn't seem to understand how it was for a woman: the giving of more than her body.

She felt for the handle of the passenger door on her side. If Damien wouldn't get out of the taxi...

'You've always avoided touching me, Natalie,' he said softly, suggestively.

'You avoided it, too,' she flung at him.

'*We didn't dare touch one another for fear of what would follow,*' he taunted her.

'I feel the same way now.'

'*I don't.*'

There was too much truth in what Damien was suggesting. Natalie felt an urgent need to escape from it. She found the handle, lifted it, and flung the door open. Before Damien could stop her she leapt out of the taxi, plunging away from him.

She heard the shout, ignored it. The screech of tyres gripping the road surface in protest she didn't ignore. She didn't see the car in the other lane. She didn't feel it hit her, and she didn't feel any pain. Violet, purple and red colours merged momentarily on her retina. She felt an impact. Then nothing, nothing at all.

CHAPTER THREE

NATALIE'S mind was definitely fuzzy. She had the sense of being disembodied. She was in a bed. It wasn't her own bed. How she knew she wasn't quite sure, but she knew.

She tried to reason out where she was and why. Nothing surfaced. Her memory seemed to have disintegrated into a jigsaw where the pieces needed to be sorted out. She gave up the effort. The thought came to her she should open her eyes and look.

She did so with some trepidation. It was a hospital bed. Tubes looped to her arm. She shut her eyes again. She'd seen enough to identify where she was. It was an intensive care unit.

Someone was talking nearby.

'...severe concussion. Brains are a bit scrambled at the present moment. Nothing broken. Nothing that won't heal properly.'

It was an affable voice, speaking with confident authority, but how dared he speak of her brains as if they were a pastiche of broken eggs!

'So the prognosis is...?'

A different voice, deeper, warmer, richer, more passionate.

'Fine. There'll be some memory loss for a short period. That will return quite naturally.'

'How long?'

'Somewhere between a few days and a few months.'

'But her memories, all her recollections, will return?'

'Without fail. Everything.'

Natalie forced a wary eye open. Who were these people who appeared to be discussing her quite openly in front of her?

The light wasn't too bad. She opened the other eye, as well. Two doctors stood at the foot of the bed.

'Ah, she's awake again.'

That was the affable voice. It belonged to a short, slightly built man with sandy hair and spectacles.

'Do you know your name?' he asked.

'Of course, I know my name. It's Natalie.'

'Natalie what?'

'It's not Natalie Watt at all.'

'Can you tell me your second name, Natalie?'

The persistent questioning made her feel very uncomfortable. She knew she knew the answer but it didn't come to mind.

'Natalie Something,' she responded irritably. They wouldn't be able to argue with that.

'That's good. Very good,' the affable man soothed.

Natalie dismissed him. She turned her attention to the other man, the one with the passionate voice. He was tall and broad-shouldered and so good-looking Natalie bet all the nurses swooned in his wake. He moved around the bed and sat on a chair beside her. He had riveting eyes, grey, with double rows of thick black lashes.

'You've had a nasty knock on the head. Seven stitches. Everything is going to be fine,' he assured her.

'I know that, Doctor,' she assured him back. She'd heard the other one say there was nothing that wouldn't heal properly.

'I'm not a doctor.'

'Who are you then?'

'I'm... Damien.'

He looked anxious, uncertain, so she smiled to put him at ease. 'Hello, Damien.'

He relaxed and took her hand in his. 'Hello, Natalie.'

He had a beautiful voice. His fingers gently stroked her palm. Her skin tingled. It was a pleasurable sensation, soothing in one way yet oddly intimate, as though he was imparting some of his own energy through his fingers. She could feel little rivulets of warmth travelling up her arm. She wondered if he had healing hands.

'I like your touch,' she said.

His face broke into a smile. His lips gave it a rueful twist but his eyes simmered with a warm

approval that seemed to zing right into her heart.
There was something very special about this man.

'Are you some kind of therapist?' she asked.

He looked at her helplessly, seemed to come
to some decision. 'I'm your lover,' he explained.
There was a blaze of determination in his eyes,
as though he wanted to sear that claim indelibly
on her mind.

Natalie stared at him in consternation. How
could she mislay a memory of that magnitude?
What was she doing with a lover anyway? Then
she recollected she was in an intensive care unit.
Only family was allowed there. Had he lied to
get in? If so, who had sent him? And why?

She looked sharply at the doctor who still stood
at the foot of the bed. Did he accept this man as
her lover? He didn't look suspicious. He seemed
to have adopted the role of interested spectator.
Natalie decided to get some facts straight.

'Where is my mother?' she demanded.

The doctor gestured to the man called Damien.
Natalie swung her gaze back to him, her eyes
sharply watchful as she waited for answers.

'Your mother's in Noosa, Natalie.'

'Did the ambulance take me to Brisbane?'

'No. You're in Sydney.'

'What for?'

'Do you remember what happened to you?'

'I had a fall in the gym. Tried a double somer-
sault over the vault.' She frowned, not quite sure
she had that right. 'Maybe it was a triple.'

'You've been floating in and out of consciousness for two days, Natalie.'

She'd lost two days of her life. No wonder they were dripping something into her arm! She couldn't comprehend why they had flown her to Sydney.

'Can I go home now?' she asked.

'If you tried to stand up you'd probably fall over. Try sitting up.'

Natalie tried and gave up without a struggle. It was easier to lie still.

'You had an accident. Your memory will come back. So will your strength.' Damien fondled her hand, pressing reassurance. 'It will simply take a little time.'

She had a very uneasy feeling about those statements. 'What's wrong with my memory?'

'What happened in the gym must have occurred years ago, Natalie. You're here because you were knocked over by a car.'

Years ago?

Her mind whirled. That couldn't be right. She stared at him, looking for some waver in his steadfast gaze. There was none. The grey eyes had more than caring concern in them. They poured a message straight into her bewildered mind. *I'm here for you. I'll look after you. I'm the rock for you to lean on.*

'How old am I?' she asked, feeling that he knew. She should know, too.

'Twenty-eight,' he said without hesitation.

He squeezed her hand hard—or did she squeeze his? Twelve years lost! She had been sixteen when she had taken that fall in the gym. What had she done with her life since then? She remembered her ambition to become an artist, as well as a great gymnast. She suspected she hadn't been much good at either.

'What kind of work do I do?' she asked, feeling an urgent need to fill in the gaps.

'You're very creative. You do graphic design on a computer. At the present moment, you've signed a contract to illustrate a children's book.'

'I must be good at it, then,' she said in surprise.

'Your work is stunning.'

The admiration in his voice gave her a deep sense of pleasure.

'Keep telling her everything that will prompt recall,' the doctor encouraged. 'The patient is doing fine. I'll leave you to it.' He gave Natalie a smile, Damien a man-to-man nod, and made a brisk departure.

The doctor's confidence was comforting. Natalie did her best to relax. She rolled the name 'Damien' around in her mind, trying to find echoes of it to patch together into a meaningful picture.

Nothing.

Yet his hand and eyes said she belonged with him, and the feeling he evoked in her suggested the same thing. She looked at him wonderingly.

She was twenty-eight. He looked to be in his mid-thirties. What precisely was their connection?

'How long have you been my lover?'

His eyes were unflinching, steely, unrelenting. 'Many years. But in all that time we never made love physically.'

'Why not?'

'You were married.'

Another shock! 'Who was I married to?'

'A man named Brett. Brett Hayes.'

His eyes were searching hers.

She looked away, disconcerted at not remembering. How could she possibly forget a husband? And a lover! She glanced down at her left hand. No rings. The hospital staff might have taken them off. She stared at her ring finger. The golden tan of her skin was unbroken by a pale band. She couldn't have worn her wedding-rings.

'Am I divorced?'

'No. Widowed.'

She felt a glimmering of memory…something coming back…something important. Her heart filled with a rush of maternal love and pride. She swung her gaze to Damien, feeling a sense of triumph. 'I have a son. A beautiful boy.'

He nodded gravely. 'His name was Ryan.'

'Where is he now?' she cried eagerly. 'Why isn't he here?'

It was Damien's turn to be discomfited. He lifted her hand and kissed her fingers, transmitting his healing warmth and a deep caring.

Then he looked at her with a sad compassion that chilled the warmth. 'I'm sorry, Natalie. There was another accident a year ago. Ryan was . . . killed.'

As soon as he said it, she knew it was true. The happiness drained out of her heart, leaving an aching, senseless void. Her beautiful boy was gone. Like the years he had occupied in her life.

Damien must have seen or felt her distress. 'That's why you want to have another child,' he said, the intensity in his voice drawing her attention back to him.

'Do I?' she asked listlessly.

'Yes. More than anything else,' he asserted. 'And I want very much to be the father of that child.'

His passion poured into the empty spaces inside her and stirred a consideration of the future. She didn't understand how he was her lover, yet they still hadn't made love together. He looked a very virile man. It must be she who was holding back for some reason.

Damien's fingers grazed longingly over hers, wanting a response from her, not demanding, but she could feel the wanting reaching into her, finding a deep chord of harmony that assured her he was speaking the truth.

She didn't know why, but the thought of this man being her lover felt . . . familiar. A sense of rightness, of contentment, swept through Natalie. Yes, she did want another child. And what better man could she choose as the father? Most women would gladly line up to have such a man as their mate.

'We're not married,' she half-queried.

'I don't think you wish to marry again.'

'Why not?'

'Your first marriage...' He hesitated. She could see it pained him to talk about it. He shook his head. 'It wasn't all you wanted it to be, Natalie.'

So that was the problem. She was wary of commitment. It wasn't exactly fair on Damien to load him with the damage caused by another man. If he had loved her for years, he had been waiting a long time for her acceptance. She should know...

'Chandler,' she said. 'You're Damien Chandler.'

'That's right.'

'And I'm Natalie Arnott.'

'Before you were married you were Natalie Arnott.'

Whatever had happened in her marriage was over, Natalie thought. Damien must be more important to her now. She had remembered his name.

'Thank you for being a nice and very patient lover, Damien,' she said warmly. 'Thank you for... for looking after me.'

His smile irradiated sunshine. 'I'd do anything for you, Natalie.'

She sighed, deeply moved by his devotion to her. The talking had made her very tired. Her eyelids closed of their own weight. She could feel the light tingling of his strong hands. It forged a bond of trust.

'I like your touch,' she reaffirmed.

Of one thing she was certain. Whatever she had been like before the accident, her instincts had been very good at choosing a lover.

CHAPTER FOUR

DAMIEN came to see her every day.

No one else did.

He brought her flowers, chocolates, fruit, magazines, highly expensive and beautifully perfumed toiletries, everything she might desire to make the hours in hospital less burdensome. She was moved out of Intensive Care after the danger of a cerebral haemorrhage subsided. In the more relaxed atmosphere of a ward, Damien's attention to her excited curiosity and speculative gossip.

That was all very fine, but Natalie wanted her memory back. Once she was out of her drug-haze from the initial trauma of the accident, it weighed very heavily on her mind that she had a twelve-year gap in her life, and she was increasingly frustrated in her efforts to recall it.

Why did there appear to be only Damien in her life? That troubled her more and more. She tackled him about it on her fifth day in hospital.

'Not one person has come to visit me except you. Do other people know I'm here, Damien? I can't remember so I don't know whom to call, but I must have some friends in Sydney.' She accepted now that she did live in Sydney, New South Wales, and not at Noosa, Queensland.

'You shut everyone out of your life when Ryan died,' he explained. 'This past year... there were friends and acquaintances who did try to draw you back into their social circle. You rejected every invitation. After a while they stopped trying and drifted away.'

She could understand their withdrawal, however regrettable she found it now. 'You're saying I isolated myself.'

'Completely.'

'Except for you.'

He gave her a dry smile. 'I persisted.'

She wondered why. She had looked at herself in a mirror. Admittedly the stitched gash on the side of her scalp didn't help her hairstyle. She did have nice eyes and a good figure, but she was not the type of woman who would automatically create a sensation wherever she went. Damien only had to enter the ward and general conversation faded out as every eye swivelled to follow him.

On the other hand, all she had to do was look into Damien's eyes to know he wanted her. Very much.

And she wanted him.

Every time she saw him she felt the strong kick of response inside her. It wasn't so much how handsome he was or how splendid he looked in his tailored suits. There was more to Damien than

superficial charisma. It was what happened between them, the tug of feeling, a response that
was evidently grounded in a long knowledge of
each other.

'I must have been a trial to you,' she stated
flatly.

He shrugged. 'You were grieving.'

For her son.

But what about her husband?

Damien wouldn't talk about him. She supposed that was natural if he wanted her for
himself. Why remind her of the man she had
married? Nevertheless, it made Natalie feel as
though she was trapped in a dark area, unable
to move forward with the confidence she should
have.

'You have a faraway look in your eyes,'
Damien observed. 'What are you thinking?'

'Speculating about the future.'

'Am I in it?'

Her eyes danced teasingly. Perhaps it was a
female instinct to like him being a little bit uncertain of her, but she quickly chided herself for
being unkind in the face of his unswerving devotion. 'How could you not be,' she said lightly,
'in some form or other?'

She expected him to smile. It surprised her that
he didn't. 'You could cut me out of your life like
this,' he said, using his finger to demonstrate
the action of a guillotine. 'You've done it
to...others.'

She winced. 'Was I so bad, Damien?'

He took her hand. His eyes were hooded as he fanned his fingers over her knuckles, arousing the sensitivity she always felt at his touch. 'We all carry some emotional baggage which turns out to be garbage, Natalie,' he said. 'At the moment, you're free of it. When your memory returns, it will colour your reactions and responses.'

'To you, as well?'

'Yes, certainly. To me.' He lifted his gaze and seared her heart with the agonised conflict that raged inside him. 'I don't want it to happen, Natalie. But it will.'

'Will it be a...bad...reaction? To you, I mean.'

He paused fractionally, then gave a firm answer. 'Yes. It will be a bad reaction.'

'So what does that mean?' she asked, perplexed.

She couldn't imagine why she should turn on this man. There did not seem to be any reasonable explanation. She waited expectantly for Damien to give her an answer. When his reply came, it was nothing she could possibly have anticipated.

'It means,' he said slowly, as if he had an infinity of pain, 'that I have limited time ... maybe ... between one or two days and a couple of months before your memory is fully restored. In that period of time I have to fulfil my life.'

The blaze of purpose, resolution and desire coming from his deeply recessed eyes lent such

impact to his words, Natalie was struck by the
need for an instant response, an assurance to him,
a defence of the fair-minded person she felt
herself to be. Through whatever eyes she had seen
him before, the man she saw now was a man she
wanted in her life.

'I don't know what you're talking about,
Damien, but I promise you this. I won't forget
what you've done for me, nor the way you've
stuck by me through everything.'

She had hoped he would relax, look reassured.
All that stared back at her was total disbelief.

'What did you do to me,' she whispered, 'that
I should respond to you...in such a negative
fashion?'

'Nothing,' he said mockingly. 'Maybe I should
have. I don't know. What I can declare with absolute conviction and honesty is that I did nothing
to you at all.'

It chilled her.

'Then what kind of person does that make
me?'

'Essentially you are the finest person I've ever
known. But you were hurt, Natalie. Dreadfully
hurt.'

'And that's what I've got to recollect?'

He nodded. 'All the doctors state definitely
that you will have total recall.'

'I don't know that I want those memories
back.'

'It's inevitable. It must be accepted.'

'What will happen to us...when I do remember?'

The alarm and concern she felt must have been written plainly on her face. Damien moved, sitting on the edge of the bed where she was propped against the tilted backrest. He gathered her into his arms, holding her close to him, tenderly, as though he treasured her.

She slid her hands around his neck and lay her head on his shoulder. They were broad and strongly muscled shoulders, made to lean on, to weep on, to rest on. As she nestled her breasts against his rock-solid chest, and breathed in the wonderful, unique scent of him, Natalie felt a comforting sense of homecoming...relief, pleasure, the sweet promise of all that was missed, and the magic of finding it waiting to be taken up again.

His fingers caressed the nape of her neck. His mouth brushed over her hair, and she was glad it was soft and silky from having been washed today. She wanted to feel perfect to him, as perfect as he felt to her. She was tempted to press her lips to the warmth of his throat, but realised this wasn't the time or the place for such an intimacy.

She felt the tension in his body, the restraint with which he was holding her, and knew he was thinking of how to answer her question about their future together, even as he imparted the comfort that he would never change.

'You will hate me, Natalie,' he said gently.

No equivocation. Forthright. Blunt. Honest.

His certainty jolted her. 'Even worse than I hated my husband?' She didn't know how she knew she had hated her husband but she intuitively suspected she had.

'I think it will be worse,' he murmured. 'Far worse.'

'Why?'

'You suspect something of me which isn't true.'

'What is it?'

'It's not a memory I want you to recall.'

'You won't tell me?'

'No.'

She lifted her head, deeply perturbed by the deadly barriers he saw coming between them. She wanted to push them away, decry their existence, but one look at the grim bleakness on Damien's face told her he had spoken the truth, a truth he hated, but one that was inescapable.

Natalie's mind suddenly latched on to the most recent event in her life. 'The accident, Damien? Why was I knocked over by a car?'

He did not flinch. 'You did not look where you were going, Natalie, because you were running away from me.'

She stared at him, thunderstruck. It was proof of what he said, yet it was in direct contradiction of the feelings he evoked in her. She struggled to make sense of it. People ran away in fear and confusion. Or when they were dreadfully hurt.

She drew back from him, instinctively reacting to fear and confusion now. Damien did not try to hold her in his embrace. He gently eased her on to the pillows, then tenderly stroked her cheek.

'I am trying to prepare you, Natalie,' he said, pained at the need, yet clearly determined not to hide behind a curtain that might be ripped aside at any moment.

He was right to do it. Yet his honesty was devastating. It gave Natalie a miserable feeling of isolation. Total isolation. Without Damien, her life would be barren of any meaningful human connection.

Where could she go?

What could she do?

CHAPTER FIVE

NATALIE fretted over her situation long after visiting hours had passed and Damien had gone. There was too much she didn't know about herself. She had to relocate her identity. It was not healthy to be so dependent on one person. She had to broaden her world.

She thought of her mother. On impulse she rang her. It was a strangely unreal conversation to Natalie. It didn't serve its purpose at all.

Her mother chatted on about what had been happening in the boutique she managed in Noosa. She told her the same kind of news Natalie had heard in her adolescence. Nothing had changed. They were simply echoes of a past long gone.

Even when Natalie mentioned her accident and the loss of memory resulting from the concussion, it was readily apparent that no help would be forthcoming in her quest to find herself. Her mother represented love and care and support, but she was too far away in more than physical distance.

Natalie ended the call, accepting the fact that her years in Sydney formed a different phase of her life, a phase she would not have confided to a parent. It was easy to share happiness and achievements. Failure was naturally hidden. Natalie was in little doubt that she must have considered herself a failure. Perhaps even as a mother. Was that why she had grieved so long, so excessively over Ryan, shutting herself away from everyone?

She searched her mind for something positive about herself.

The answer finally came to her.

It was in her handbag.

The one concrete fact connected to both her past and future was the signed contract for her work on the children's book. She didn't know why she had been carrying it with her on the day of the accident, but it represented something she had achieved.

Natalie took it out to look at it again. The contract contained her home address and the publisher's address. Attached to it was a covering letter from an editor who wrote enthusiastically about Natalie's work. The name signed at the end of the letter was Sharon Kippax.

Surely she must have met Sharon Kippax if they were doing business together. It might be worthwhile meeting her again, talking to her. It would be an opportunity to gauge another person's reaction to her, even if it was only that of the slimmest acquaintance.

Resolution formed in Natalie's mind. Tomorrow she would release herself from the hospital and pay her publisher a visit. Although she was bruised and sore, and a little shaky on her legs, she was not so weak she couldn't manage to get around by herself. There was nothing really wrong with her, except for the intimidating gap in her memory.

The fearful thought struck her that she might not be able to fulfil the contract. Had she forgotten the skills needed to produce what she did? Would her work still be as 'stunning' as Damien said it was?

She fought the fear down with an even firmer resolution. There was no point in worrying about it. She would find out tomorrow. It was time to take a step by herself, for herself. No running away. No sheltering behind Damien's devotion to her. She had to go out and meet the world she occupied head on.

The next morning Natalie discovered that signing herself out of hospital was a tedious business. They didn't think she was ready to leave, so every obstacle was put in her way.

She had the feeling that Damien could have achieved the same result in half the time, but Damien was at work, and she couldn't call on him for *everything*. Besides, she took some pride in proving herself capable of handling and overcoming the difficulties she met.

When she was dressed, packed and ready to leave, she did call the number Damien had given her. A secretary informed her, 'Mr Chandler is at a business meeting.' Natalie left a message for him that she had left the hospital, then set off to accomplish what she could alone.

The taxi from St Vincent's Hospital deposited her outside a tall office building in North Sydney. The directory in the foyer listed her destination as the fourth floor. She caught a lift. When the number four flashed up, she picked up her suitcase, ready to step out. The doors opened.

A woman was waiting to step in. She wore a striking yellow suit with black accessories. Her hair was black, her eyes dark, and she was beautiful.

I know her, Natalie thought with a little spurt of excitement. The sense of triumph was dashed when the woman stepped briskly into the lift and pressed a button, giving Natalie no more than a cursory glance in passing. There was not the slightest flicker of recognition in her eyes, no smile of fellow acknowledgement.

Natalie quickly propelled herself out of the compartment, embarrassed by her expectation and the dismissive manner of the other woman. Yet her inner certainty that they were not complete strangers made her turn to glance questioningly at the woman again. Did she know her or didn't she?

The woman returned a preoccupied look. The lift doors closed, putting an end to the odd encounter. It niggled at Natalie's mind as she walked over to the receptionist's desk, and continued to niggle throughout her meeting with Sharon Kippax.

The editor was in her twenties, cheerful in nature, and immediately sympathetic to Natalie's plight. She showed Natalie a portfolio of what she had submitted. Natalie couldn't help feeling a thrill of pride in the striking flights of fantasy she had produced. She really did have talent!

Sharon went through what had been planned for the children's book. She was kind, patient and as helpful as she could be, but she struck no chord of recollection in Natalie.

It wasn't that Sharon had a nondescript appearance. She had friendly hazel eyes, a mass of curly brown hair, and an attractive, expressive face. Natalie instinctively liked her.

'Have I been difficult to deal with?' she asked bluntly.

'Not at all,' Sharon replied reassuringly. 'You've been as eager about the project as I have. I love your work. It's creative. I truly don't think you have anything to worry about. Once you sit in front of the computer again...well, it's like reading. You haven't forgotten how to do that.'

Natalie hoped it was a valid point. 'Have we met often?' she asked, fiercely wishing she could remember.

'No. Only three times.'

'I'm sorry I can't recall you. The doctors do say it's only a matter of time.'

'Please . . . don't distress yourself. I'm sure it will all come back to you.'

'There was a woman getting into the elevator. She wore a yellow suit. Very smart . . .'

'My boss. Project manager.'

'What's her name?'

'Anne Smith.'

Natalie sighed. It didn't mean anything to her. 'It's hardly possible to get a more prosaic name than that,' she remarked ruefully.

'Believe you me, Anne Smith is not a prosaic person,' Sharon said, rolling her eyes at the comment. 'She's a human dynamo. She's not only on the ball all the time herself, she expects everyone else to be. In fact, it was Anne who spotted the work you submitted. Instant decision. "Get this person under contract,"' she mimicked, then smiled. 'She has a great eye for spotting talent in every form.'

'She wore black when I met her,' Natalie said with gathering certainty.

Sharon frowned. 'But you've never met.'

'We've *never* met?'

'My orders were to handle this project myself. Completely. Anne's kept right out of it. You've never met.'

'That's extraordinary! I was so certain . . .' Natalie dismissed the idea for the time being. Perhaps her memory was playing tricks on her.

Sharon, she thought, might become a friend in time. She felt the liking was mutual. Apart

from that, she did have something to do, and
something she did well. What Sharon had shown
her of her work had convinced her of that. It
gave her a pleasant sense of satisfaction and
autonomy.

She caught another taxi to her home address
at Narrabeen. It was a beach suburb on the north
side of Sydney Harbour, which probably explained her tan, but Natalie felt cold inside when
she saw the house she lived in. A double garage
faced on to the street. A high brick wall hid the
rest, giving the place a shuttered, unwelcoming
appearance.

She found the key to the locked gate in the
brick wall on her key-ring. She walked slowly
down a side-path that led to a covered porch protecting what was obviously the entrance to the
house. Natalie automatically chose the right key
for the door.

She stepped into a large open-space living area,
very modern, and furnished in a style she knew
instinctively was not her taste. She eyed with a
sense of disbelief the glass and chrome tables,
the leather sofas and chairs, the lack of any
colourful character.

She dropped her suitcase and shoulder-bag in
the entrance foyer and walked over to the glass
doors at the far end of the living-room. Beyond
them was an extensive patio and a swimming-
pool. No lawn. No garden. A few landscape-

designed areas with palm trees and ferns for shade.

An expensive house in an expensive location, she thought, and wondered about her finances. Was there a heavy mortgage on this property or was it paid for? Had her husband been a high-income earner? Had they led a very social life throughout their marriage?

She trailed slowly through the house, room by room. The furnishings were basically neutral, smartly fashionable, ultra-modern, without any striking individuality. Show-rooms, she thought, finding it difficult to accept she had lived here without wanting to change anything, or at the very minimum add some personal touches. Hadn't she cared about her surroundings? Had Brett insisted on this sophisticated but soulless lifestyle image?

Why had she continued with it after his death? Why hadn't she sold the house and made a different home for herself somewhere else? Had she simply stopped caring about anything? Even the study where she obviously worked on the computer was functional rather than personal.

What must have been Ryan's room had been stripped of any evidence of childish occupation. No nursery things. No toys. No remembrances at all. Maybe they were shut away in the cupboards. Or had she been unable to bear reminders of what was forever lost and given it all away to a charity?

Natalie found her tour of the house unutterably depressing. If this represented her past, she felt no kinship with it. Perhaps, if she opened the cupboards, went through the drawers, some sense of familiarity might return. There had to be mementoes of her life here somewhere. But she didn't feel capable of continuing her search. The purpose that had fired the day's activities drained into a flood of exhaustion.

Her legs finally carried her back to the master bedroom where she flopped weakly on to the king-size bed. She managed to work off her shoes and drag some pillows out from under the quilted cover. She was trying to settle herself comfortably on her side when she saw the photograph.

Her heart lurched.

Ryan.

A golden little boy framed in gold.

The photograph stood on the bedside chest of drawers, turned to face where she lay. Natalie's hand automatically reached out to bring it closer to her.

He was laughing, his sherry-brown eyes sparkling with delight. He had a soccer ball clutched in his arms, and he wore a red tracksuit and navy blue sneakers. The background was a park she didn't recognise, but she remembered how Ryan loved playing with balls and balloons: kicking them, catching them, throwing them, bouncing them.

A happy child, giving happiness. Poignant memories flashed into Natalie's mind: Ryan splashing joyfully in a bath, squealing excitedly as she swung him out and bundled him into a towel, holding him close, smelling the sweet clean freshness of his skin and hair; Ryan uninhibitedly snuggling up to her, saying, 'I love you, Mummy.'

Natalie hugged the photograph to her as she lay back and closed her eyes, savouring the pictures that slipped into her mind. Ryan, taking his first steps towards her, the surprise, the glee that he could do it shining from his eyes; the joy of riding his tricycle on his second Christmas; the pride of achievement when he learnt to swim... 'Look at me, Mummy!'

I couldn't have been a bad mother, Natalie thought with heart-lifting conviction. My boy meant the world to me. My son...Ryan...

Chimes echoed through the house, insistently calling for her attention, too many chimes for it to be a clock. The doorbell, she realised, shaking herself out of the doze she had drifted into. The doorbell could only mean Damien. She had shut everyone else out of her life.

The framed photograph of Ryan slid off her stomach as she pushed herself up from the pillows. She picked it up, gazed sadly at the laughing little boy, then reinstated the golden memory where it had sat on the chest of drawers.

It wasn't a piece of celluloid she needed to hold, but a live flesh-and-blood child.

The door-chimes called again.

She fumbled her feet into her shoes, raked her fingers through her hair, then made her way out to the foyer to let Damien in. She opened the door and was instantly subjected to a concentrated scrutiny from caring grey eyes that bored into her soul, filling the emptiness there.

'Are you all right, Natalie?'

She nodded. 'Come in, Damien.'

His glance fell on her suitcase and shoulder-bag as he entered. 'You haven't been here long?'

'Long enough.' She closed the door, then gestured sweepingly at the living rooms open to view. 'This...doesn't feel like home to me.' She searched his eyes, anxious for the answers she needed. 'What was I like...as a person?'

'On the day you were married you were filled with joy and love and laughter, brightly anticipating all the good things in life. You were...' his voice softened, deepened '...the most desirable woman in the world.'

'You were there...on my wedding-day?'

'Yes.' His mouth took on an ironic twist. 'That was when I met you for the first time.'

'What did I become, Damien?'

'Withdrawn, introspective, unresponsive. No smiles for anyone...except Ryan. This past year you've been sullen, morose, isolated and alone. People could talk to you and were ignored. I doubt you knew they were talking to you, myself included.'

'Why did you put up with it?'

'Who wants to see a candle snuffed out? A flower that fails to bloom?'

She shuddered at the images evoked. 'I don't like this house,' she cried. 'It's... it's sterile. It isn't me, Damien. If it was, I don't want it to be me any more.'

'What do you want, Natalie?' he asked softly.

She went to him unhesitantly, her hands resting lightly on his chest, her eyes imploring his for understanding and acceptance.

'Take me away from here, Damien.'

His arms came around her, drawing her closer. 'Yes,' he said simply.

She leaned on his wonderful strength, laying her head contentedly on his shoulder. She felt his chest rise and fall. A long breath wavered warmly through the short waves of her hair. She didn't know or care where Damien would take her. She wanted the candle to burn brightly, and the flower to bloom, and she wanted to be with the man who believed it was possible, who had cared enough to wait to see if it would happen.

CHAPTER SIX

DAMIEN took her to his apartment.

It overlooked the ocean at Collaroy, not far from Narrabeen, yet the moment Natalie stepped into Damien's living-room she was in a different world from the one she had once inhabited.

Warm, welcoming, earthy and sensual were the words that sprang to mind. The carpet was the colour of candied honey. Big squashy sofas were upholstered in a fabric that combined green and orange with leopard and zebra prints. The parquet top of a large square coffee-table fascinated with its unique design. A smaller mobile table supported a television set.

Set into a recess was a cabinet for stereo equipment. A rack displaying a range of compact discs rose above it. Bookshelves holding an extensive private library stood beside a nook accommodating a well-stocked bar. Oak and brass dominated. Wooden stools were softened by tan leather seats.

In front of the floor to ceiling windows overlooking the sea views was an informal eating area: a round cane and glass table with four tub chairs softly cushioned in the same fabric as the sofas. The adjacent kitchen featured oak cupboards, polished granite bench-tops, and a luxuriant potted fern spilling its long fronds over the divider from the dining setting.

Natalie was intrigued by what was revealed of Damien. He enjoyed comfort, liked a touch of the exotic, and was used to pleasing himself. He was methodical, tidy, had a place for everything, and everything in its place, yet that did not detract from the welcoming atmosphere. This was very much a home, a highly individual one, and Natalie felt a sense of privilege at being invited into it.

'Have I been here before?' she asked.

'No. This is the first time,' he said softly, as though it was a momentous occasion for him, the end to years of waiting and wanting.

Natalie's heart contracted at all she had put him through, however unwittingly. She swung around to face him. He had set her bags down near a hallway and was observing her reaction. She smiled her pleasure at being in such a user-friendly place.

'Was it because I always refused any invitation? Was I being remiss?'

He shook his head. 'You were never invited.'

So bringing her into his home was a decisive step for him, laying himself open to her as he had never done before. He didn't look vulnerable in her opinion. There was an air of lonely pride about him as he waited to see how receptive she was to the situation. It was as though he was saying to her, This is the man I am. I want you to stay but the choice is yours.

'I'm happy to be here,' she assured him, 'and your sofas look very inviting.' She gave a rueful sigh. 'I'm afraid I'm about ready to wilt.'

He visibly relaxed and gestured her forward. 'Make yourself at home. Have you had anything to eat?'

'No. I didn't think of it.'

'I'll get you something in a moment.'

While he took her bags to another room, Natalie slipped off her shoes and gratefully sank into the deeply cushioned corner of one of the sofas. She lifted her legs up and settled herself comfortably. Her body ached. She was exhausted. Too much in one day, she thought, although she did not regret any of the steps she had taken.

Damien returned, divested of most of his business suit. His shirt collar was opened, his sleeves rolled up. Clearly he intended relaxing with her. He gave her a smile of approval as he passed by, leaving her to rest quietly while he went to the kitchen and set about making coffee and sandwiches.

Natalie watched him, marvelling that *she* had some special appeal to him. Many women must have crossed his path over the years, and he was far too attractive not to have been pursued by some. It seemed unreasonable to her that he should have reached his mid-thirties without forming a serious attachment to anyone else. Yet she looked around her and saw entrenched self-sufficiency. There was not one sign of female companionship present.

He brought her a plate of ham and cheese and lettuce sandwiches. Natalie found she was hungry and ate with appetite. Damien settled into the sofa opposite her, content to sip his coffee and wait until she was ready for conversation.

'All the time I was married...you couldn't have remained celibate, Damien.' She was curious to know more about him.

'I tried to get you out of my mind,' he said drily. 'I wasn't notably successful at it.' There was a hungry look in his eyes, softened by the prospect of the intimate togetherness her presence in his apartment promised.

'What about before that?' Natalie asked.

'I was married.'

It surprised her. She felt uncomfortable with the idea of Damien's having a wife, a woman he must have loved and lost. She sternly reminded herself that she had lost a husband. Had Damien's wife died, too?

'What happened?' she asked.

He shrugged. His expression changed to a world-weary cynicism. 'I suppose you could say everything or nothing. We ended up wanting different things. As it turned out, divorce was the only thing we shared. Or had in common.'

He must have been hurt by it, Natalie reasoned. No one could fail to be hurt by the crumbling of a commitment that was entered into with deep emotional involvement. 'I'm sorry,' she said with sincerity and sympathy.

He shrugged, as though that segment of his life no longer had any relevance to him.

'How long were you married?' Natalie asked, slightly disturbed by his apparent nonchalance to the severing of vows that, to her mind, should never be taken lightly.

'Three years.'

'Any children?'

The hungry look swept back into his eyes, sharper, more intense than before. 'None.'

Was that an intrinsic part of her attraction for Damien—her love for Ryan and her desire for another child? He had made no secret of his desire to be a father. It was a natural biological urge. Natalie certainly had no quarrel with it. She knew intuitively she would have little in common with a man who didn't want a family. Damien wanted what she wanted. She breathed a sweet sigh of contentment. It was a relief to know there were no children hurt by his divorce.

'Where is your ex-wife now?' she asked, wondering if the past was completely cleared away for him.

'She's the feature editor for a national women's magazine.'

He made it a simple factual statement, without any trace of judgemental opinion in his voice. Not that Natalie expected any from Damien over a woman's career.

'Are you on friendly terms?'

He toyed with his coffee-cup, then looked at Natalie in the most direct fashion. 'Lyn was a lovely person. Later, she changed. I deeply regret what happened between us. It was unnecessary, ineffectual, and in a word... stupid. But it did happen.'

'I'm sorry. I didn't mean to intrude on something so private and personal...'

'I rarely see Lyn any more,' he continued, determined on answering the questions she had raised. 'The difference between us was one of priorities. She now has a live-in relationship with a made-to-order television journalist. It seems to suit her. They've been together for a few years. On the surface they appear to be happy. If that's what she wants... I'm content to let the matter rest.'

Two journalists involved in demanding careers, no time for children, Natalie thought. Everyone was entitled to their choice of lifestyle, and if being free and unencumbered suited them best, that was fair enough. Damien was right. He accepted the separation between himself and his wife and whatever pain he had suffered at the time of their divorce was long since gone.

Natalie wondered how she'd feel when she remembered her own marriage, then quickly shuffled the thought aside. She had no right to judge Damien on whatever hurt she had suffered through another man. She felt a strong surge of conviction that Damien was the right man for her, right in every way. She didn't want her present opinions clouded by what was best forgotten.

She frowned over this last thought.

'Something wrong?' Damien asked.

'It occurred to me that I might have a subconscious wish to block out my memory of Brett.'

He said nothing. His face tightened fractionally. His wife might be in the distant past but clearly the spectre of her husband stirred raw feelings.

'Can you respond to me as I feel now?' she appealed, wishing she had not reminded him of Brett.

'What do you want?'

She laughed at herself. 'I'm too tired to move, yet there's a restless urge inside my mind. I feel I want to go somewhere but I'm not sure where it is or why I want to go there.'

'Well, we could try looking for it tomorrow,' he said obligingly, but she sensed his disappointment that she was not content to simply remain here with him.

She leaned forward impulsively, wanting him to know she cared, wanting him to understand, searching her mind to explain more clearly what she felt. 'Let us go somewhere together. Somewhere... to start afresh.'

The desire that flashed out at her was hot and urgent and barely controlled. She was suddenly, painfully aware of how sorely she had tried his patience, how frustrated he must be in still finding her elusive. A flush of guilt and shame pulsed into her cheeks and she looked away, struggling to justify her decision to follow her own instincts instead of considering his needs.

'Whatever you want, Natalie,' he conceded gruffly. 'You are like a will-o'-the-wisp...'

His voice trailed away. She understood perfectly what he meant. She could not afford to keep him waiting too long without running the risk of forfeiting everything. Her gaze flew back to his in apology.

'It sounds so selfish after all you've done for me.'

He shook his head. 'I did what I wanted to do. You owe me nothing.'

The self-mocking look in his eyes hurt. How many rejections had he suffered from her?

'You look worn out,' he said flatly. 'I'll show you the bedroom. Let you get some sleep. Tomorrow is another day.'

He pushed himself up from the sofa, rounded the coffee-table, took her hands and helped her onto her feet.

Tomorrow, she thought. Will I be different tomorrow? Will I remember things that appear to be best forgotten?

He led her into what was obviously the master bedroom. Her bags were already there.

'You'll find the en-suite bathroom through that door,' he said matter-of-factly, pointing it out to her.

'Where are you going to sleep?' she asked, turning to him with anxious eyes, not wanting to disappoint, ready to agree to whatever he wanted even if she wasn't fit to do much more than lie in his arms.

'There's a divan in my study.'

Her hand fluttered to his chest in both appeal and protest. 'I don't want to turn you out of your bed, Damien.'

He touched her cheek tenderly. 'You need a long rest, Natalie. You wouldn't get it if I were in bed with you.'

His hand dropped to her shoulder and trailed slowly, caressingly down her arm, transmitting a need to touch that quivered through her skin. She saw the conflict rage in his eyes, felt the tension of fiercely imposed control.

'This may not be very appropriate action right at this moment,' he said huskily, 'but I've been waiting a long time.'

His hands enclosed her waist with a steady, sure, purpose. His eyes were locked on to hers, compelling her acceptance. The powerful force of his desire stirred a turbulent restlessness inside her. She didn't know if she moved towards him or he towards her. Her hands slid over his shoulders, around his neck. Her head tilted back. She felt her body poised for what was coming, every nerve alive with anticipation. Her lips parted.

His mouth seemed to explode into hers with a hungry passion, wild for the taste of her, demanding a response that matched his need. From deep inside Natalie came an overwhelming surge to satisfy him, to please herself, to lose herself totally in the excitement of knowing all they were capable of feeling together.

Fatigue was forgotten. If there was pain from her bruises when Damien pressed her closer to him, she didn't feel it. She was completely possessed by the yearning to feel his body against hers. She revelled in the hard strength of him, the power that embraced her, enveloped her, kept her captivated in absolute thrall to the sensations he aroused.

Her head swam with the intoxication of a kiss that was no mere mingling of mouths. It was a fierce claim on all that she was, a driving, heart-pounding, unbridled search for what was, and what could be between them, a giving and taking that sent streams of exultation bursting through her. Yes, she wanted this. Yes, she wanted him. All of him. Yes, it felt wonderfully, beautifully, gloriously right. He was the man for her, the man

who could share this with her and so much more.
She wanted everything.

Natalie was still awhirl in her vibrant inner
world when Damien started to draw away from
her. Not abruptly. His lips lingered over hers. His
arms relaxed to a gentle hold. His hands caressed, no longer pressing her to him. He lifted
his head and she heard his fierce intake of breath,
felt the swell of his chest.

It took her several moments to realise he didn't
intend to go on. Dazedly she opened her eyes.
She had no idea what he saw in them, but in his
was a look that seared her soul, compelling recognition and acknowledgement of what had just
happened between them, and for which he had
been waiting all these years. She belonged with
him. To him. He would not accept anything less,
and from the response he had drawn from her,
the response she had ultimately and uninhibitedly given him, he had every right to expect it
to be the same in the future.

He *knew*. The knowledge blazed in his eyes.

He said nothing.

Natalie could not find her voice to speak.

There was no need for words anyway.

He *knew* and she *knew*. The knowledge
throbbed between them, irrefutable. They were
in intimate accord in wanting each other. There
could be no going back to whatever their relationship had been before the revelations of
those last few moments.

He stepped away from her, his arms dropping to his sides. She stared at him, realising he meant to leave her alone in his bedroom to rest, to wait for tomorrow. She almost cried out for him to stay, yet in some strange sense the knowledge was enough for now.

She watched him go, watched the door close behind him. The last door, she thought. Tomorrow they would go away somewhere together and there would be no doors between them.

Except the door to her memory.

But it wouldn't matter if that opened or remained shut, Natalie decided confidently.

Damien Chandler was the man for her, and nothing could shake or change that decision.

CHAPTER SEVEN

'NORTH or south?'

Damien's question was accompanied by a smile. It was evident he didn't care where they went. His eyes glowed with anticipation for what would come at the end of their journey. In the meantime, they were together, sitting side by side in his car, ready to leave for whatever destination Natalie chose.

She wasn't quite sure what prompted her reply. It did not come from any urge to be contrary. 'West,' she said decisively, answering some strong intuition that no other direction would serve the need she felt to find a special place.

'You want to go to the Blue Mountains?'

Was it surprise that wiped out Damien's smile, or did he dislike her choice?

'Do you mind?'

His eyes quickly scanned hers. 'Of course not.' He dismissed the question.

She shrugged. 'I don't know why, but it feels right.'

'Whatever you want,' he said, nodding agreement as he started the car.

Natalie relaxed contentedly as the powerful engine thrummed into action. The lambswool

75

seat-cover was heaven to sink into. The Jaguar SL suited Damien, she decided. Sensual comfort and high-level performance. A ripple of excitement spread through her at the thought of how he would translate both those aspects of his character into lovemaking. Or would the wild passion he had briefly unleashed yesterday slip out of his control?

She looked at the hands guiding the steering-wheel, strong, capable, yet so knowingly sensitive in their touch. Her gaze drifted to his muscular forearms, left bare by the navy and cream T-shirt he wore, then dropped to his powerful thighs where the denim of his blue jeans was tightly stretched. Was it the casual clothes that made her more physically aware of him, or was it the memory of how his body had felt pressed to hers?

She studied his profile. What woman wouldn't find him attractive? How was it possible she could have been unmoved by his pursuit of her before the accident? Natalie shook her head in helpless bemusement. She must have been a blind fool.

It was a beautiful day, brilliant sunshine from a cloudless blue sky, a day befitting the start of something new. Natalie sighed her satisfaction. She might not know precisely where she was going, but she was certainly in the right company.

'Is being with me causing any problem with your business, Damien?' she asked, struck by the realisation he would normally be at work since this was a weekday.

He laughed. 'I wouldn't care if it did.'

'That's rather a cavalier attitude for the boss of a company, isn't it?'

'*You* are more important to me.' He slanted her a sizzling look that made Natalie's skin tingle with heat.

There were years of frustration behind that look. With fulfilment of his long repressed desires in the offing, Damien was not about to let anything get in his way. Natalie couldn't blame him for the attitude. Patience did have its limits, and Damien felt pressured by the threat of her hating him when she remembered all there was to remember.

Was she being reckless in taking this plunge with him now?

Natalie squashed the thought, angry with the doubt, determined to trust her feeling for him no matter what eventuated. Damien had sworn he had done nothing to deserve her animosity and she believed him. She must have been dreadfully twisted up inside to have misjudged him so badly. She would get the misunderstanding sorted out when her full memory returned.

The choice to head towards the mountains should indicate something about herself. She searched for a memory that made sense of it. She suddenly recollected being a tourist guide at Noosa, taking people on bush-walks through the national forest and...yes...to the Glasshouse Mountains, so named by Captain Cook because of their conical shape. She had always enjoyed those day-trips.

The Blue Mountains to the west of Sydney were a long way from south-east Queensland, but Natalie was sure the peaks and cliffs and valleys would have a similar appeal to her. It definitely felt right to go there.

Satisfied she had made a relevant connection, Natalie was smiling happily to herself when other images of the past flashed into her mind: painting in her spare time, mostly landscapes that were readily saleable at a price most people could afford. She had been quite good at capturing a scene, although far from being an outstanding talent. Of course, it was much easier to experiment with colours and different palettes on the computer. It was marvellous how the whole aspect of a picture could be changed and polished in a manner no traditional artist would attempt.

It surprised and delighted Natalie that these last thoughts followed on so naturally. It boosted her confidence in her ability to fulfil the contract with her publisher. Sharon Kippax was right. The knowledge was there in her mind to be tapped when she was ready to start again.

'Have you met Sharon Kippax, Damien?'
'Never.'

'Do you know anything about children's books?'

'Only what I remember from my childhood.' He gave her a reminiscent smile. 'My mother used to read to us every night. Bedtime stories were a ritual. I think they're great for kids.'

The warmth in his voice reminded her of his desire to have a child of his own . . . with her. She formed a mental picture of Damien reading a book she had illustrated to their children, pointing out Mummy's vision of the story with pride and love. It tugged on her heart, making it ache with longing.

She could not remember her own father. He had been killed in a cyclone trying to help other people to safety. She had been only two years old at the time and her mother had never remarried. Natalie had envied her friends who had fathers and brothers and sisters. It was no fun being an only child and she now recognised that her mother had not found it easy being a single parent.

'Do you come from a big family?' she asked.

'Three boys, two girls.' He grinned at her. 'I was the youngest, but we were all close. Most of the kids in the neighbourhood came to our house to play. I had a great childhood.'

'Tell me about it,' Natalie prompted.

He recounted a series of wild adventures and outrageous mischief. It seemed that his parents had adopted a policy of free rein, occasionally pulled in with some salutary discipline when the line of acceptable behaviour was flagrantly over-stepped. They were an achievement-orientated family, seeking to stretch their horizons and go wherever their interests took them.

Damien's amusing anecdotes kept Natalie interested and entertained through the trip across the city to the foot of the mountains. He fell silent as they started the climb upwards.

Natalie was hard-pressed to keep the conversation flowing. She found out Damien's oldest brother was a pilot working for Singapore Airlines. His other brother was a marine biologist, based in Tasmania. One sister lived in London, having gone to England on a working holiday and found employment as a nanny for the children of a widowed stockbroker whom she subsequently married. The remaining sister had gone to New Zealand, become involved with the women's movement, fallen in love with a sheep farmer, and had settled happily into farm life, breeding Galloways as a sideline.

Damien's parents had retired to the Gold Coast of Queensland years ago. They now enjoyed a life of leisure in the sun.

'So you're the only one left in Sydney,' she mused.

'Yes.'

'You must miss them.'

'We keep in touch. Mostly when Christmas comes around.'

Christmas was for families, Natalie thought, and especially for children. It was now the month of March. By next Christmas she would be twenty-nine.

'How old are you, Damien?'

'Thirty-four.'

If they were to have a family together, their first child could be born by next Christmas. Natalie was about to act on impulse and reach across to Damien when a familiar landscape caught her eye.

'Oh! Take the left turn before the overhead bridge,' she urged quickly.

Damien gave her a sharp and penetrating glance. 'Does this mean something to you?'

'Yes...no...I don't know.' The question flustered her because she had no ready answer to it. 'I just feel this is the way to go.'

He took the turn. 'The road leads to Leura.'

It meant nothing to her. They had left the outskirts of Sydney some considerable time ago and she had only been vaguely aware of travelling up the freeway to the mountains since then. Whether they had reached the top of the range or not she had no idea.

They approached a fork in the road. A signpost to Leura pointed to the right. 'Keep left,' Natalie said automatically.

Damien frowned at her. 'You remember being here before?'

'Not really. I don't understand it but I feel sure this road leads somewhere I want to go.'

It was a long road. They passed signs to two vacation resorts, one longstanding, one new. Damien gave her a run-down on their facilities. Neither of them had any instinctive pull on Natalie. They passed golf links. Then she saw the row of pines, thickly clustered to close out the rest of the world.

'That's it!' she cried excitedly.

'What?'

'There's a gateway between the pines. It has an arch. You'll miss it if you go quickly, Damien.'

He slowed down. He turned the car into the driveway and brought the car to a halt. On the arch was printed the name of the property, 'MERLINMIST'.

It had to be a magical place to be called that, Natalie thought, feeling certain it had the special quality she had been seeking.

'What does Merlinmist mean to you, Natalie?' Damien asked, his eyes fastened intensely on hers, almost accusing. The tension emanating from him bewildered her.

'Does it mean something to you?' she countered.

He made a visible effort to relax. 'I've never stayed here.'

'But you know of it.'

He nodded. 'It's listed as a boutique guest-house. *Haute cuisine*. Four guest suites, each one uniquely decorated. Very exquisite. Very exclusive. Very expensive. Very, very expensive. The gardens and trees were planted forty or fifty years ago by Hildegard, a famous landscape artist. I believe the outlook over the Jamieson Valley is quite spectacular, something any artist would want to paint.'

'You must have been here before to know all that,' Natalie said, disappointed he had already shared it with someone else.

'No, I haven't,' he repeated. 'I've heard about it. Many times.'

Her heart lightened. 'Is it too expensive for us?' she asked warily.

'Not for you.'

'I'd like to stay.'

'Natalie...' he seemed to struggle with some inner conflict '...you said you wanted a fresh start together.'

'This is the place, Damien,' she assured him. She must have seen it before, gone past it perhaps, and been so drawn to it that the wish to stay had lingered in her subconscious memory, a special place for a special occasion. 'Every instinct I have tells me it's right,' she added with conviction.

'Instinct...' A look of savage irony flitted over his face.

'What's wrong, Damien?' she asked anxiously, aware that her choice did not meet his whole-hearted approval.

'You're the only one who can make the decision. If you say it's right, it's right,' he said decisively, shrugging aside whatever doubts he'd had. He gave her a rueful smile as he reached across and took her hand. He interlaced his fingers with hers. 'We're together. Nothing else is more important to me.'

Natalie was intensely relieved at his surrender to the compulsion that had selected this place above all others. Yet she could not easily dismiss the tension flowing from him. His fingers gripped hers tightly, impressing his need for her. She wanted to say nothing else was important to her, either, but it wasn't true. For some inexplicable reason, she needed Damien to share Merlinmist with her.

He withdrew his hand, and with an air of determination drove into the parking area for guests. The house was large, solidly built in red brick, two-storeyed, many-chimneyed, and with an impressive pillared portico protecting its entrance. It gave the sense of having stood the test of time, built to last against adversity. It had an instant and deep appeal to Natalie, as though it represented all she had lost, or all she was looking for in her new life.

Damien nodded to the three other parked cars as he helped Natalie alight from his. 'We could be disappointed,' he warned. 'They might be fully booked.'

'Fate wouldn't be so unkind,' she declared, her eyes alight with confidence as she curled her arm around his.

He smiled at her but he was still tense. She wished he would relax and enjoy the moment. The air was crisp and cool and invigorating. She felt brilliantly alive. Nothing could possibly go wrong. They were going to have a wonderful time together.

A honeymoon, she thought.

Merlinmist was the perfect place for a perfect honeymoon.

CHAPTER EIGHT

THEY were lucky. There had been a late cancellation. One suite was available until the weekend. Three days and nights in this marvellous place, Natalie thought triumphantly. It was more than enough.

She loved the smell of beautifully polished furniture, loved the glorious floral arrangement in the foyer, loved the grand mahogany staircase that led upstairs, loved the dignified and gracious atmosphere that came with tall ceilings and panelled walls and richly patterned rugs and carpets.

Her eyes sparkled with excitement as she was ushered into the bedroom she would share with Damien. Her gaze was immediately drawn to the magnificent half-tester bed that dominated the décor. Its yellow drapes looked stunning against a padded bedhead upholstered in a striped floral pattern. The detailed designer fabric was repeated in the valance below a white quilt on which were piled a liberal adornment of yellow and white cushions.

The night-stands on either side of the bed were matching Victorian sewing tables on graceful three-legged pedestals. They held tall brass lamps with yellow shades. Natalie swung around to see what balanced this splendid grouping of furniture. Facing the bed was a majestic chest of drawers with a large mirror, reflecting it all, giving double the visual pleasure.

She turned to look at Damien, hoping he was favourably impressed. She saw only the back view of him as he followed their hostess past the green velvet armchairs flanking a wide hearth. At the end of the sitting area, a log fire was set behind a glass-fronted fireplace. Damien adopted a listening pose as he was told how it worked, then crouched down to open the door and set the logs aflame.

Natalie's attention wandered to the far wall where an elegant *chaise-longue* was placed in front of the windows. It provided casual relaxation for the viewing of winding valleys and spectacular red and yellow ochre cliff-faces that stretched as far as the eye could see.

A shiver ran down Natalie's spine. The sheer stone cliffs looked so stark above the blueness of the eucalypts massed below them, stark and...unforgiving. She frowned over that fanciful last word. It was silly to attach any emotion to a geographical phenomenon.

She quickly responded to their hostess's invitation to inspect the en-suite bathroom. Damien stayed behind to watch the progress of the licking flames, apparently intent on ensuring that the fire, which was rendered unnecessary by the air-conditioning system, made adequate progress.

Natalie had the feeling that Damien did not know what to do with himself, but any activity, no matter how intrinsically useless, was preferable to doing nothing.

The bathroom was as splendid as everything else. Walls of gleaming white tiles were topped by a blue and green ceramic frieze, making a highlighting feature of the blue and green and yellow towels. The floor inside the shower stall repeated the colours in foliage tiles to match the frieze. A spacious spa bath added the ultimate touch of luxury.

Natalie made appropriate comments to their hostess who nodded her satisfaction and waved Natalie back to the sitting-room. A porter brought up their bags. A maid carried in a tray holding a crystal bowl of sultana grapes and strawberries, a bottle of champagne in a silver ice-bucket, and two fine flute glasses. She placed it on the table near the armchairs. Their hostess informed them lunch began at one o'clock should they wish to use the dining-room. The business of getting settled was finally completed, and Natalie and Damien were left alone in their suite.

Damien stood with his back to the fire, as though he needed warmth. There was a strained look about his face, a watchful reserve in his eyes. He made an effort to smile. 'A fine room,' he said.

He seemed to be waiting for her to take the first step. It was her choice of setting, her insistence that had brought them to here and now. Natalie wondered if she had made a mistake in taking the initiative away from Damien. Did he feel she had her priorities wrong? Was he keeping himself aloof in expectation of another rejection?

She recalled him saying as he acceded to her wish to stay at Merlinmist that the decision was up to her. This was decision time, too. He had told her what he wanted with her. He could not have spelled it out more clearly. Only she was important. The surroundings meant nothing.

'Thank you for indulging me, Damien,' she said softly, dismissing the attractions of this unique guest house as she walked across the room to him, her eyes locking with his in compassionate understanding of the dilemma he faced... whether or not to take what he most wanted while she was willing to give herself to him. The temptation must be tearing him apart, aware as he was she might hate him for taking advantage of the present situation.

'I want you to be happy with me,' he said with heart-tugging simplicity.

'How could I not be when you give me so much?'

There was anguish in his eyes.

Natalie lifted her hands to his chest. She could feel his heart thumping madly under her palm. She tried to impart reassurance, confidence. 'I trust what I am now, Damien, not what you tell me I might become. If I'm going to change, I want you to feel fulfilled with me now. Let this be my gift of love to you. Forget all that's gone on in the past. Feel only this.'

She slid her hands up to draw his head to hers and she pressed her lips fervently to his, wanting to give flesh-and-blood reality to her words. His arms came around her, crushing her to him as his mouth began to move over hers in a yearning kiss that ignited a flood of desire.

She felt the tense urgency in his body, the need that strained against the soft pliancy of her stomach, stirring an ache deep in her womb. She opened her mouth, inviting the passionate force she had tasted yesterday, exulting in the wild mutuality of their hunger for each other.

Kissing wasn't enough. Holding wasn't enough. She rubbed her breasts against the hard muscles of his chest, wishing it were flesh to flesh. Damien's hands slid to her buttocks, squeezing them possessively as he thrust her closer to the pulsing surge of his need.

His mouth left hers. His chest heaved for breath. She opened her eyes, hot liquid amber, burning with the fiery mission to complete what had been started. Somewhere in the back of her mind was a sense that it had started a long time ago, started but been kept rigidly hidden behind doors she had locked. Whatever had simmered so long between them was loosed now, free to find the satisfaction it craved, and she fiercely wanted what Damien promised her, the ultimate height and depth and breadth of intimacy that was possible for a man and a woman...this special man and herself...together.

She saw the leap of recognition in his eyes, a wild glitter of elation at her uninhibited desire for him. He released his physical hold on her. It wasn't needed. There was another stronger bond pulsing between them, an elemental certainty. There would be no turning away from this final revelation of all they were to each other.

Damien tugged her shirt free of her jeans and began unbuttoning it.

'Take yours off first so I can touch you,' she said huskily.

He did so with a happy chuckle. It was the first sound of happiness she had heard from Damien. It swelled her heart and made it pump faster. She grazed her fingertips down the cords of his throat, across his broad shoulders and down his strongly muscled arms. He was beautifully made. Her man, her mate, she thought with such primitive satisfaction that it made her acutely aware of the basic drive that brought men and women together.

Damien peeled off her shirt, removed her bra. His hands cupped her breasts and he gazed down at them as though enthralled by their womanliness. Was he thinking they were made to give succour and comfort, to pleasure him in the ways men found pleasure in their shape and softness? She felt her nipples harden. Damien inhaled deeply and lifted his eyes. Natalie's breath caught at the look of tenderness in them.

'You touch my needs more deeply than anyone I've ever known,' he said softly, then bent to take her breasts in his mouth, sucking them in turn, sending deep shafts of pleasure through her body, tapping a well of love so strong she found herself cradling his head, stroking his hair, wanting to hold him to her forever.

But he slipped away from her, kissing her stomach as he knelt to remove the rest of her clothes. That gave her a different pleasure, both shivery and molten, the soft, warm brush of his tongue stroking her naked flesh, the sensual caress of his hands on her thighs, behind her knees, her feet.

She reached for him as he rose upright, her hands feverishly ready to strip his manhood bare, to make him feel valued and cared for and cherished. His skin quivered under her touch as she freed him from constriction. His fingers twisted convulsively through her hair as she trailed her lips over the swollen life force of his flesh, cupped and gently squeezed the potent pouch that held his seed ... for fathering a child.

He moaned her name in an ecstasy of longing and she rejoiced in his need for her, his pleasure in what she was doing. She drew rippling patterns over the powerful muscles of his thighs, feeling them tighten to rock-hardness as she cleared them of the clinging fabric.

Then he was helping her, freeing himself so he could scoop her up and hug her body to his, his mouth invading hers with urgent passion as he carried her with him to the bed. He hurled the quilt aside and laid her on the cool sheets. He loomed over her, then pulled himself back, arching in anguish as he realised what had been forgotten.

'Natalie...'

'Throw caution to the wind, Damien,' she urged, wanting him to embrace their union in all its totality, flesh to flesh, pulsing life to pulsing life.

'Yes...' He expelled the word with a violence of feeling that expressed a turbulent inner world of pent-up emotion. She saw his control disintegrate, torn asunder by a raw blaze of male possessiveness.

He drove himself deep inside her and she wrapped her legs around his hips, rocking with him in a rhythm that beat into her mind and heart and soul, a pounding crescendo of ecstatic fulfilment as they claimed each other in a mating ritual as old as time. She loved the solid strength of him plunging to her womb, tried to hold him clasped there, to restrain the passage of his withdrawal, exulted as he thrust forward to fill the waiting void again. Her whole being centred on the sensation, and the excitement of it multiplied, peaked, and burst into a molten mass of exquisite pleasure.

She heard Damien cry out, felt the wild strain of his body still pulsing inside her, then his climactic release spilling another flood of warmth, mingling with hers, forging the ultimate completion. His arms burrowed under her, hugging her close, carrying her with him as he rolled on to his side, enveloping her in a cradle of intimacy that held them joined together.

His hands moved caressingly over her in a blind fervour of touching. He kissed her hair, his lips skimming sensually over its soft silkiness, savouring the freedom to taste and feel in the blissful knowledge that she belonged to him as wholly and solely as he belonged to her.

Natalie lay contentedly in his embrace, her head upon his shoulder, basking in the vibrant warmth of their intimacy, feeling an incredibly sweet sense of security. We were meant to come together, she thought in languid pleasure. She had been right to abandon the past and take the future Damien offered her. Everything felt right with him.

She had no inclination to speak. The silence was beautiful, peaceful, imbued with a harmony that words couldn't express. Eventually she had to move to ease her leg. Damien was quickly solicitous of her comfort, piling pillows for her head, dragging the quilt over her to ensure she didn't become cold.

His eyes were soft, telling her how special she was to him. She smiled and trailed her fingers down his cheek, wondering if he was as sensitive to her touch as she was to his. There was still so much to learn about him.

'Tell me what you feel,' she said impulsively.

'Joy.' He grinned. 'I am literally tingling with a wild effervescent pleasure I can barely contain.'

She laughed from sheer elation that he felt the same fulfilment she did. 'You don't have to contain it, Damien. We can do whatever we like.'

'What would you like?'

It was typical of him to consider her feelings first. Natalie thought for a moment, wanting to please him. 'Let's have some champagne. I think we should celebrate.'

'That certainly suits my mood.'

'Stay here.' She stopped him from moving. 'I'll get it. We'll drink it in bed.' Her eyes danced wickedly at him. 'I love this bed. Especially with you in it with me.'

He laughed, his exhilaration bubbling over.

Natalie flung the quilt aside and sashayed down the room to the sitting area, deliciously aware that Damien's eyes were glued to every feminine curve of her body. It was highly stimulating to know he found her so desirable and Natalie was proud of the fact she had kept her figure in good shape. She took immense pleasure in his watching her. It was a measure of her sense of security with him that she could feel so uninhibited about her nakedness. Not only uninhibited, she found herself revelling in it.

She carried the ice-bucket back first, nestling it in the quilt beside Damien. He was propped up on one arm, a delighted grin fixed on his face, his eyes sparkling with happiness.

'You could busy yourself with the cork,' she admonished.

'I can't take my eyes off you.'

Natalie had no argument with that. She made a return trip for the glasses. The way Damien's eyes feasted over her breasts and hips and thighs was very tantalising. She decided they would forget about lunch altogether. Champagne and grapes and strawberries were fine. And seductive. And exciting. And fun.

She set the glasses on the closest night-stand and started back for the bowl of fruit. 'We might as well be totally decadent,' she declared. 'You can feed me strawberries while I'll arrange little morsels for you.'

'I feel my appetite stirring,' Damien said, the tone in his voice clearly intimating food was not on his mind.

Tucked into the side of the bowl of fruit was a grey card embossed in gold. 'MERLINMIST' was printed on it in Roman calligraphy. It was so beautifully done, Natalie automatically picked the card up and opened it to look at what was inside. '*Compliments of the house*' was printed in the same script. Her eye, however, was drawn to the hand-written message underneath.

'*Thank you for staying with us again.*'

It was signed by the manager.

Natalie frowned over it.

'What's the matter?' Damien asked.

She looked quizzically at him. 'You did say you hadn't stayed here before.'

It arrested Damien's full attention. 'That's true.'

'But I have?' It was more a statement than a question. Memories were starting to come back.

Damien looked like a man who had discovered a treasure at the end of the rainbow, only to see it summarily snatched away.

'Tell me the truth, Damien,' she demanded, but she already knew the truth. As he did, too. 'When did I stay here before?' she asked accusingly.

His face tightened into grim resignation. His eyes dulled with weariness. 'On your honeymoon,' he replied, each word a heavy drip of despair. 'On your wretched honeymoon with Brett.'

Natalie shuddered as the apt description struck home, stirring all the memories of painful confusion and disillusionment that summed up her honeymoon with Brett. The revelations rebounded on the intimacy she had just shared with Damien. She suddenly felt dirty and shamed and hurt and wounded. The compulsion to cover her nakedness was compelling, overwhelming.

She whirled and almost ran to the bathroom, remembering the robes hanging behind the door.

She couldn't bear to hunt the floor for her clothes. Such a reminder of her utter abandonment to Damien Chandler was humiliating. In *this* place... of all places! How could she have chosen it?

'Natalie...'

She ignored the imploring call, plucking a bathrobe from its hook, frantically pulling the belt apart, thrusting her arms into the long floppy sleeves, wrapping the heavy towelling fabric tightly around her in a fierce need to be properly covered.

But there was no hiding from the man who had brought her here, the man she had shared a *honeymoon* bed with, the man whose influence was so pervading and inescapable. She stepped out of the bathroom, her head tilted high, her hands thrust into the deep pockets of the bathrobe.

'Yes,' she said bitterly. 'It was a miserable honeymoon with Brett. As miserable as any woman could have. And apart from Brett himself, you had more to do with it, Damien, than any person alive.'

She glared at him, her mind flooded with black resentment of the perfection he had promised. 'How can you ever be forgiven?'

CHAPTER NINE

DAMIEN'S expression underwent a profound change. His eyes kindled with fiery determination. He rose from the bed with all the bristling pride of a man whose honour had been challenged. He was totally unconcerned by his nakedness as he strode down the room. He scooped his jeans from the floor and drew them on as though girding his loins for battle. Steely grey eyes pinned Natalie to where she stood by the bathroom doorway.

Not that Natalie wanted to move any closer to him. Damien Chandler had a lot to answer for. Outrage burned through her stomach, turning the desire she had felt for him to blistering bitterness. He had known what memories Merlinmist held for her, and he had let her make the decision without saying a word to stop or discourage her. Had there been some lurking subconscious thought that she would regain her memories in such a horrible fashion? What kind of man did that make him?

'Now, tell me, Natalie...' he stood with his arms hanging free, his torso bare, aggressive in its raw muscular power '...what possible blame can you lay at my door for what happened on your honeymoon with Brett? I wasn't here. I am not responsible for...'

'You *were* here,' she cut in fiercely. 'Every minute of every day you were here. It was because of you Brett chose this place for a honeymoon. Not to please me, but to best you, Damien. He beat you so he could boast about it to you.'

'That is not...my...fault,' Damien bit out, his eyes as sharp as scalpels, intent on slicing to the heart of her retreat from him.

She gave a bitter laugh. 'I hated you before I came to know you.'

'What did I do to deserve such prejudice?' he demanded.

She stared at him, her mind tunnelling back to her wedding-day... Brett's best man...his best friend and business partner...Damien Chandler...charming, courteous, faultlessly correct in his behaviour towards her, yet holding an aloofness that denied her entry into his personal world. That hadn't worried her at the time. She had had Brett. At least, she'd thought she had Brett. She didn't know then that Damien was the centrifugal force around which Brett's life spun, that she was a pawn in a competition, giving Brett a leading edge over Damien.

'You knew all about it, Damien,' she stated with unequivocal conviction. 'You knew Brett a lot better than I did.'

'What a man knows of another man is not what a woman knows of him, Natalie,' he argued. 'From what Brett told me, you were the perfect woman for him, and from what I observed on your wedding-day you were very much in love with him.'

'But that wasn't all you observed, was it?'

There was a flicker of evasion in his eyes. 'What are you referring to?'

'You knew what a womaniser Brett was. He didn't even have the discretion to keep by my side at the wedding reception. The only time you engaged me in conversation, at length, was when Brett went missing with one of your married friends. You should remember her, Damien,' she said with biting sarcasm. 'I asked you her name. It was Rhoda Jennings.'

'She was... the wife of a friend,' he replied stiffly. 'A gushing flirt... particularly after a few drinks. She meant nothing to Brett.'

'You covered up for him. You deliberately moved in and covered up for him while he... *bonked* is the word, isn't it?... another woman on our wedding-day.'

His head jerked in a pained negative. 'I couldn't believe he'd do it. I still don't know if he actually did. Why would he do such a thing when he had you?'

'You stopped me from looking for him.'

'I wanted to protect you from any needless upset. Brett had finished with Rhoda months before. Slipping off with her could have been a stupid impulse he'd quickly think better of. I hoped . . . it worried me . . . but I didn't know for certain, Natalie.'

'You protected him. Or tried to. You were two of a kind . . .'

'I disagreed violently with some of the things Brett did.' Damien was clearly disturbed by the course the conversation was taking. 'But I don't feel I have to disown someone because I violently disagree with them.'

'When Brett undressed that night, the musky smell was unmistakable and pervasive. He explained it away, saying it was desire for me. I wanted to believe it . . .'

'For God's sake! Why not believe him? Why on earth would he want anyone else?'

'No doubt it gave him a kick, a perverse pleasure, leaving you on Best Man duty while he lived dangerously. Thanks for looking after my bride, Damien. I'll be having her for seconds. Is that what he said to you when he came back?' Natalie couldn't keep the scorn from her voice. 'I married a creep who didn't have one faithful bone in his body.'

'You married a man with a serious problem. The way he was brought up by his father after his mother deserted them . . . it was an ingrained attitude, Natalie. He never learnt how to relate to women except in the most basic biological fashion. I thought once he had a wife . . .'

'You saw him go with that woman. You helped him all the way.'

A flush of anger speared across Damien's cheekbones. 'I knew *you* meant more to him than any other woman who'd crossed his life. I gave him the benefit of the doubt. I didn't ask what he'd been doing, and he didn't tell me. He was very attentive to you when he returned. I thought everything was all right.'

He sounded sincere. Passionately sincere. Natalie hesitated, wondering if she was doing him an injustice. Perhaps he hadn't realised Brett had been using her in a game of one-upmanship with his best and oldest friend. Yet how couldn't he know? The cruel game must have been going on for years...women, places, sporting activities, business...nothing was excluded.

Natalie wondered if Brett had deliberately kept her away from any contact with Damien while he courted her, always flying up to Noosa, never asking her to visit him in Sydney. Was getting himself a wife some kind of coup over Damien, who had lost his through divorce? Or had Brett been ensuring there was no competition over the woman he had chosen to marry?

The first time she and Damien had laid eyes on each other was in the church, moments before the marriage ceremony had begun. She remembered thinking what a contrast they were, Brett with his golden good looks and sky-blue eyes, his best friend darkly handsome, thick black lashes shadowing deeply set eyes. They had looked so striking, standing together. Then Brett had smiled at her, a bright dazzling smile, and Natalie had forgotten the man at his side.

She didn't know then she would be endlessly reminded of Damien throughout her honeymoon, that he was ever-present in Brett's psyche, dominating what should have been an exclusive sharing with her.

'I wasn't enough for Brett,' Natalie stated bluntly. 'Apart from whatever he did with Rhoda Jennings, we were no sooner here than he started eyeing the wife of another guest, playing up to her, openly flirting. He had to be the king-pin, organising outings, making each night a party. And your name was a constant accompaniment to everything that pleased him. Damien will be green with envy when I tell him about this. Damien, Damien, Damien...'

Her eyes flashed intense bitterness. 'You were more important to him than I was. Everything was more important to him than I was. It was as though he had won a cast-iron possession so he didn't have to work at giving me his undivided attention any more.'

'I'm not clairvoyant, Natalie. When I saw you walking up the aisle to Brett, I thought him a very lucky man. I thought he'd appreciate his luck.'

'So you helped his luck along,' she mocked. 'Was it a score to you when you told him you'd saved his marriage from being over before it started?'

'I've explained why I did what I did,' he snapped.

'But you called my honeymoon with Brett *wretched*, Damien. How would you know it was *wretched* if you truly believed everything was all right between me and Brett? Brett would never have told you it was *wretched*, and I would never have admitted it. Especially not to you.'

'No, your loyalty to Brett was absolute,' Damien retorted savagely. 'You never admitted anything. You shut me out as though I were a leper.'

'So how did you know?' she challenged.

'Your honeymoon...your honeymoon with Brett...was wretched *for me*, Natalie.'

The pain in his eyes stabbed her into silence. She had been so focused on what had happened between her and Brett that she hadn't considered Damien's feelings about their marriage.

'Because Brett had beaten you?' she asked.

His mouth twisted in disagreement. 'There was no contest in my mind. You had chosen him. You were my best friend's *wife*. I had to accept that. But I couldn't help wishing I'd found you first. I couldn't stop myself from thinking of you...with him...wondering if it was good...and wishing it were me.'

The passion in his voice shattered the defences she had raised, yet still she felt the need to clear the tangle of doubts in her mind.

'Did you think you might get what you wanted without my remembering? Was that it, Damien? You decided to risk staying at Merlinmist to fulfil what you couldn't have before?'

'It was *your* choice, Natalie. I acquiesced. I didn't like what was happening.'

He turned aside, scooped up his shirt, and pulled it on. He picked up his shoes and socks, sat down in the closest armchair and proceeded to finish dressing himself, doggedly ignoring her presence although the tension between them was palpable.

'I asked you what Merlinmist meant to you. You should have told me,' she fired at him, angered by his dismissal, and the truth contained in it.

'I didn't want to remind you.' He stood up, his eyes glittering resentment. 'Why the hell should I remind you of what Brett did to you? What *he* did. Not me. I never did one damned thing to hurt you. Ever!'

'You went along with my choice of staying here, knowing it might hurt me,' she returned hotly.

'What did I *know*, Natalie? *You* directed us here. *You* insisted every instinct told you it was right. I believed in your instinct. This was where you wanted to be with me. To start afresh.' He made a derisive sound. 'What choice did that leave me?'

She had to acknowledge he hadn't liked it, but did that excuse his acquiescence?

'For all I knew,' he continued bitterly, 'you had a need to wipe out unhappy memories, overlaying them with good ones. I was the one who had to stop myself from being haunted by the ghost of Brett. And now you throw him in my face. Well, if this is some twisted revenge for your twisted perception of me, I can do without it.'

She was abruptly presented with his back as he strode towards the door. 'Where are you going?' she cried, suddenly torn by the fear of him leaving her.

'To get some fresh air.' He wrenched the door open, then halted his exit, his gaze sweeping back to her, piercing in its intensity. 'Why you would want to pollute what we just shared together is beyond my understanding.'

Before she could muster any reply, he stepped out of the room and closed the door firmly behind him. As a parting shot it was deadly, sinking home the fact she was destroying the present with a past that could only poison any chance of happiness.

She lifted shaky hands out of the robe's pockets and rubbed at her forehead. What Damien said was true. He had been answering her needs in coming here, doing what she asked. She had urged him all the way. But why had she connected Damien so strongly to Merlinmist? More than that. To a *honeymoon* at Merlinmist.

All those years ago, had she ended up wishing it were Damien with her, and not Brett? Had she been playing out a secret fantasy in bringing Damien here? Or had she felt he owed her the kind of honeymoon she should have had?

She shook her head. What had happened wasn't his fault. Damien was right about that. None of it was his fault. He wasn't responsible for what another man did. Yet somehow she couldn't quite banish the feeling that Damien was some dark Macchiavellian figure behind all of Brett's actions. The dominator. But that might only be the sheer strength of his character and personality. Could he be blamed for simply being the man he was?

Natalie tottered over to an armchair, shocked at such devastating revelations about herself. She sank into the soft cushions, grateful for their support as she tried to sort through the turbulence in her mind.

Damien had predicted this violent reaction to him, the surge of hatred that would be blind to all he'd done for her, all he felt for her. It shamed her that he'd been right. He didn't deserve it. Damien hadn't forced her into anything. He had simply been there for her. Maybe he had always been there for her... throughout her marriage to Brett. Although she hadn't recognised it. Lovers, he had said, but not in the physical sense. How much frustration was there in that?

Her body clenched at the memory of their intimacy, desire so strong it blotted out everything but their driving need for each other, the fulfilment of a wanting that couldn't wait any longer. And it had been good. More than good. Wonderful. Incredibly perfect. Why couldn't she hold on to that and put the past in the past? She had to learn how to let go. Why was she afraid to accept what she had shared with Damien at face value?

Damien claimed he had never done anything to hurt her. She had no real evidence to the contrary. But it sat uneasily on her that he had been Brett's best friend...his business partner... inextricably linked to her rotten marriage. Her hatred of him...was it the other side of love? Had it been her defence against the feelings Damien stirred within her?

If only she could remember more. The years following on from her honeymoon were a grey blur. She couldn't pluck anything out of them except Ryan, the precious child she'd loved and lost.

Ryan... Her gaze drifted to the window... the unforgiving cliffs on the other side of the valley. She felt the blood drain from her face as understanding drove through her mind. Ryan had fallen over a cliff, fallen to his death...and Brett had died, too, trying to save Ryan...but too late...too late...

Damien was mixed up in those events somehow. Damien, covering up for Brett, always covering up. She couldn't trust Damien. She didn't know what went on inside his head, what his real feelings were. He only told her what he deemed it necessary for her to know within the ambit of their relationship. While he might have spoken the truth, was it all the truth?

She didn't know. She simply didn't know. And she was afraid of what she didn't know. One thing she was certain of. She couldn't stay here with Damien now. Merlinmist was too tainted with memories that neither of them would be able to dispel.

She considered what course of action she should take. She needed time to fill in the gaps in her memory. If her perception of Damien was twisted, as he claimed, she wanted to get to the heart of the matter, and she couldn't do that until she knew more.

She didn't feel up to travelling far, didn't want to go back to the sterile house she had shared with Brett. She remembered the name of one of the resorts they had passed on the way here. Fairmont. A few days there might provide some answers. She could hire a car or take a train when she was ready to return to Sydney. Since Brett had been Damien's business partner, she must have some money, although a memory stirred that there had been financial difficulties.

Having made her decision, Natalie pushed herself into moving. She telephoned the Fairmont Resort. There were rooms available. She booked one for a week. Satisfied she had a place to go to, she showered and dressed. With one last regretful glance around the room that had seemed so warm and welcoming, she picked up her bag and went downstairs. Perhaps one day she and Damien might return and know lasting happiness in the half-tester bed with the yellow drapes. She thought not. The ghosts of yesteryear were not so easily exorcised.

She left her bag at the reception desk in the foyer and went outside in search of Damien. She had to speak to him first before calling for a taxi. She checked the parking area. His Jaguar was still there. She walked around the grounds, barely noticing the artistry of the landscaping, not pausing to read the plaques on the magnificent specimen trees. Damien was nowhere to be seen.

She took the zigzag path that led down to the valley far below. She hoped Damien hadn't gone far. She didn't have the strength for a strenuous walk. She paused at the first bend, watching the mist swirling up from the valley, obscuring the view. What she needed was Merlin's magic to dispel the mist in her mind. If only it could be that easy.

She plodded on with a heavy heart, not anticipating any joy in meeting with Damien, but she couldn't run away from him. He deserved an explanation from her. An apology, as well. She had to be fair. In her ignorance, she might be doing him an unjustifiable injury in not accepting what he held out to her.

He was sitting on the garden bench at the third bend. He was not looking at the view. He was hunched over, elbows resting on his thighs, hands linked between his knees. He didn't hear her approach, too absorbed in his thoughts to be aware of anything outside them. He looked weary beyond measure.

Natalie's heart squeezed with painful uncertainty. Had she tried him too far? Was she a fool to hesitate over joining her life to his? Would she lose what she wanted through doubts that had no substance?

'Damien...'

His head jerked up and snapped around. It was plain he was startled to see her. Not expecting it. Not expecting anything from her. He rose to his feet in a slower movement, gathering his emotional resources to deal with whatever came. She could sense him arming himself and wished it didn't have to be that way. If only they could go back...retrieve the heady freedom of having no emotional baggage from what had previously happened. But it hadn't been that way for him, and now it couldn't be that way for her.

'I'm sorry I acted so...so unkindly,' she offered, feeling hopelessly inadequate to express herself.

'It was always going to happen, Natalie,' he stated flatly. 'I knew it...yet I can't accept it.' His eyes searched hers for some latitude. 'Are you staying or fleeing?'

No attempt at persuasion. Her choice would tell him all he wanted to know.

'Damien, I'm very attracted to you...'

He made a sound of deep exasperation. 'Is this the overture before I get the "Can we be good friends?" speech?'

She flushed. 'I can't afford another mistake like the one I made with Brett.'

'Can't you trust your instincts, Natalie?' he burst out, his eyes blazing with the need she had fed so recklessly.

'My instincts led me into marrying Brett,' she cried, more in protest at what Damien stirred than with any logic in her argument. 'I need some distance to get everything in proportion.'

'You had everything in proper proportion when you couldn't remember anything.' His hands lifted in a gesture of urgent appeal. 'Stop listening to your mind. Go with what you feel. Come to me.'

'I can't. Not yet. Please...' She stepped back, fighting the strong tug on her heart. 'I'm asking you to wait, Damien.'

'Wait!' His face twisted with feeling. He fought to control it but it throbbed through his voice. 'How long, Natalie? How long am I to wait this time? Until you have another car accident? Another lifetime?'

'Until I believe what you tell me.'

It silenced him. He arched his head back as though she had hit him with an uppercut to the jaw. Then slowly he turned to look out over the mist. 'Will-o'-the-wisp,' he muttered. 'You'll bracket me with Brett until the day you die.'

That could be true. Natalie had no answer to it. She'd had a rotten husband, and for all she knew, Damien had been aiding and abetting Brett in his infidelities, perhaps encouraging him to do what he'd done, wanting her to find out, wanting her to turn to him, wanting to win out in the end. Or was that a twisted reaction from the miserable life she had led?

Who else knew Damien intimately? Who could tell her what he was really like to live with?

The answer came immediately.

His wife. His ex-wife. Lyn. It should be easy enough to find a Lyn Chandler who worked on a woman's magazine.

'Give me a month. I need that to get my bearings, Damien. I promise I'll give you a definite answer then.'

He turned to her with a gaze that seared her soul. 'What if you've conceived our child today, Natalie? Will I be told?'

Her stomach contracted. 'It won't happen. I'm sure it won't.'

'But if it does?' he insisted.

'You'll be told,' she heard herself say. The consequence of throwing caution to the wind was that she could end up with a child whose father she did not wish to marry or live with. 'You'll definitely be told,' she repeated, but her lips trembled.

She turned and headed up the path, trepidation for the future in every step. It was vitally important that she remember everything, vitally important to question Damien's ex-wife. She had to know what kind of husband Damien had been, and why the only thing he and his wife had shared in the end was a divorce.

CHAPTER TEN

NATALIE spent five days at Fairmont. It was a fine, impersonal place for her to rest, eat well, exercise in the heated indoor pool, and take long leisurely walks. The room service was excellent, the amenities first class. She didn't seek company and no one pressed company upon her.

She tried very hard to marshall all the facts she knew and make some consistent order of them. Bits and pieces of her four years of marriage to Brett came back to her, and she tried to take a more objective view of her husband, and why he was the way he was.

He had taken her home to that house in Narrabeen. It had already been furnished by a 'first-class' interior decorator, and Brett was intensely proud of it. No way would he countenance any change.

He had been generous with money, encouraging her to buy 'first-class' clothes and whatever added dignity and status to their lives. She was the woman in his home, his wife, the artist, the mother of his child...all images that reflected well on him.

It was important to Brett to be perceived as a man who had the best of everything.

Damien was right about Brett's not relating to her, or any woman, as a person. She had never connected that aspect of Brett's character to his background as Damien had. She had viewed their upbringings as something they had in common, both of them only children, cared for by a single parent.

Yet hadn't not having known a father influenced her to stay with Brett despite her personal unhappiness? She hadn't wanted Ryan to be without a father, and Brett had been very good with Ryan. Perhaps as his father was to him.

If attitudes and values came from family background, then what of Damien's? Surely, with his happily married parents and an ample number of brothers and sisters, he should be a well-rounded person, confident of holding his own anywhere and in any company. That was the way he came across. Perhaps Brett had seen Damien as the man who had everything, someone to pit himself against to be at the top.

Precisely how did Brett and Damien relate? They had certainly meshed in their computer world. Perhaps it was difficult to find people who could connect compatibly within that specialised type of field.

They both enjoyed the same athletic activities. They were both popular at parties, though different in the way they performed at them.

Damien tended to have conversations. Brett specialised in witty repartee. Damien engaged people's interest. Brett made them laugh.

Of course, that was why Damien was so good at making deals. He listened. Brett skated over the surface in talking, but he skated it so brightly, no one seemed to notice any shortcoming in depth. It was Damien with the depth.

He and Brett complemented each other in many ways. Alike, yet not alike. That was probably the basis for a strong and lasting friendship, but they were *not* two of a kind. Natalie came to the strong conviction she had been wrong in holding that point of view.

It could very well be that it was only Brett who had been obsessed in competing with Damien, while Damien felt no sense of contest at all, only companionship.

And loyalty.

Not by word or deed had Damien ever indicated he coveted his friend's wife while Brett was alive. Perhaps that was why she had never been invited to his home. On the other hand, not by word or deed had he ever indicated she had good reason to divorce Brett. Not to Natalie's recollection.

She could not make up her mind if this implied his attitude to women was the same as Brett's or not. Perhaps he'd considered Brett's wife untouchable, but he had certainly touched other women, and all of them, to her knowledge, only short-term affairs. Like Brett.

Was it true that none of them had measured up to her in Damien's mind, or was that an excuse for his brief dalliances?

Natalie caught a train back to Sydney on Monday morning, and spent the entire two-hour trip wondering how to approach Lyn Chandler. Over the weekend she had looked through the staff lists of several women's magazines, checking the names of the features editors until she found Lyn Chandler's place of work. It struck her as odd that the woman had not reverted to her maiden name after the divorce from Damien. The more she thought about it, the odder that circumstance appeared.

Somehow she had to persuade Damien's ex-wife to meet her and talk about the marriage that had only lasted three years. It would be a revealing key to Damien's character. Or to Lyn Chandler's. Natalie was sure of it.

She wondered if her graphic design work might interest a features editor. A professional approach might be best. After so many years' separation from Damien, his ex-wife might be totally uninterested in any personal angle that involved him. Although anything could come out in a face-to-face chat. After all, Natalie had been the wife of Damien's business partner. Lyn Chandler had to have known Brett before he married Natalie.

Since Natalie could now relate the house in Narrabeen to her life with Brett, she could walk into it without it worrying her. After unpacking, she hunted through the desk in her office and found a portfolio of her work. She hoped it was impressive enough to give substance to a business meeting.

She telephoned the magazine's office just before twelve o'clock, hoping to catch Lyn Chandler at a free moment. She was in luck. She was put through to the features editor with no trouble at all.

'Natalie Hayes!' a bright voice exclaimed. 'You wouldn't happen to be Brett Hayes' widow by any chance?'

'Yes, I am,' Natalie affirmed, surprised at the other woman's instant connection of her name to Brett.

'Damien and I were talking about you only the other night. You're illustrating children's books now.'

'Yes.' Natalie barely got the word out. Damien had given the impression he was out of current contact with his ex-wife.

'Well, good for you!' Lyn Chandler said warmly. 'Losing both Brett and your son was a terrible tragedy. Must have been devastating. Brett was so full of life. A wonderful man.'

'Yes,' Natalie agreed faintly.

'I dare say you don't want to talk about that but I wanted to express my sympathy. Now, what can I do for you, Natalie? I may call you Natalie?'

'Of course.' Natalie was stunned by the open friendliness being offered. 'I wondered if I might interest you in the kind of work I do. Perhaps run a feature on it as a career choice. If we could set up a meeting...'

'Great! How about four o'clock this afternoon? I'm free then. Does that suit?'

'Yes. Thank you.' Natalie was begining to feel like a gasping fish, stunned by the ease with which everything was being arranged.

'If you're not busy afterwards, perhaps we could follow up with a few drinks and a bite to eat somewhere. I might be able to give you some good contacts for placing your work.'

The offer was so incredibly obliging to Natalie's needs, it raised the question if Lyn Chandler wanted something from her. Nevertheless, it was an opportunity too good to miss. 'That's very kind of you.'

'Not at all. I was very fond of Brett. Great as a party guy. I'm well acquainted with how lonely it can be on your own.'

'Thanks, Lyn. Whatever you suggest is fine by me.'

'OK. I'll look forward to meeting you at four. Just ask at the front desk and they'll direct you to my office.'

'Thanks again.'

Natalie sat in a daze, wondering what was going on. Lyn's friendly attitude couldn't be Damien's doing. He would have no reason to suppose she would get in touch with his ex-wife, no reason to ask any favours for her sake. Lyn had to have reasons of her own for setting up a social get-together.

Which brought Natalie to the loaded question... had Damien deceived her about his current relationship with his ex-wife? What had been going on there, between the brief affairs he'd had with other women?

She frowned, wanting to believe what he had told her. Perhaps their recent meeting was one of the rare occasions he had mentioned. Natalie told herself she would find out soon enough, so there was no point in worrying about it.

Female pride prompted her to dress and groom herself to her best advantage. She was going to meet a woman whom Damien had presumably loved. Not that she was competing, she told herself severely, but she would feel much more confident if she looked good. Professional. The white linen suit was simple and elegant and shaped very nicely to her figure. Natalie was satisfied it was an appropriate choice for the occasion.

At four o'clock she was ushered into a work-efficient office that was crowded with filing cabinets and a large desk loaded with stacks of folders. Lyn Chandler looked very much at home in a hive of industry. She radiated vitality as she rose to greet Natalie.

She was a chic blonde, her hair cut in a short, fashionable bob that suited her pretty face. Deep dimples in her cheeks somehow made her smile infectious. Her eyes were striking: large and long-lashed, with light green irises ringed with brown. She was tall and slender and looked very stylish in a form-fitting beige skirt and tan silk blouse. Her perfume was more spicy than floral, a sharp rather than a soft scent, perhaps an assertive statement that she was a woman who chose not to conform to others' expectations.

Natalie had no problem imagining any man being attracted to Lyn Chandler. She would light up anyone's life with her smile. She also exuded warmth and caring interest, so much so that Natalie couldn't help thinking it had to be Damien's fault that the marriage had broken up.

Lyn enthused over Natalie's portfolio and asked a lot of questions, drawing her out about previous artwork, training, ambitions, and the children's book she was illustrating. She made notes and expressed the opinion that an article could be worked around unusual art-forms and the women who were creating them. Natalie could expect a follow-up call for an interview when arrangements were made.

Business satisfactorally completed, Lyn invited Natalie to share a taxi to the Intercontinental Hotel, where they both relaxed in the Cortile, a casual lounge area where both snacks and drinks were served and background music was supplied by a pianist stroking the keys of a grand piano.

Lyn ordered two gin and tonics, two double brandies, and triple vodkas. Natalie swallowed her astonishment and made no protest, although she privately considered so much alcohol excessive. It might, however, loosen Lyn's tongue, which was all to the good.

A dish of mixed nuts on their table provided nibbles. Natalie scooped up a few cashews, biding her time until the drinks arrived, making appreciative comments on the décor around them. The waiter returned with their order. Lyn disposed of her gin and tonic as though it was lemonade. Natalie decided this was as good a time as any to open the conversation she wanted.

'I didn't know you saw much of Damien any more,' she prompted.

Lyn laughed lightly. 'Oh, I saw him as recently as Saturday. Damien always has time for me. I needed a shoulder to cry on. My *ex*-live-in and I had a fallout.'

'I'm sorry to hear that,' Natalie said sympathetically, hiding her unease at the familiarity that apparently remained between ex-husband and ex-wife.

'He is now definitely *ex*,' Lyn said with satisfaction. She smiled. 'It makes a difference to Damien.'

Natalie tensed, unable to control the alarm that shot through her heart. Had Lyn been using her live-in lover as some kind of lever to wring some concession from Damien? She sipped her gin and tonic, refraining from comment, waiting for Lyn to elaborate.

'I could never rely on Julian for anything,' she said, shrugging a contemptuous dismissal of the man she had lived with, 'and I'm tired of always having to manage everything for myself. I now realise I need someone solid and dependable and stable. Like Damien.'

'You mean . . . financially?'

'That, too. But other aspects have priority now.' Lyn picked up her glass of brandy and sipped it. She looked speculatively at Natalie as though sizing her up. 'I don't mind getting back with Damien,' she stated with cool deliberation. 'There's still that spark of attraction between us. And now that he's selling his business, he'll have the time necessary for me.'

Natalie barely veiled her shock. 'I thought you must have been disillusioned with your marriage to Damien. Wasn't it you who commenced the divorce proceedings?'

'I thought marriage to Damien was going to be fantastic. It was for a while. Mr Perfect, you know? I was madly in love with him.'

'So what went wrong?'

She laughed easily. 'He had the bad habit of working long hours, and taking business trips at the drop of a hat. I felt neglected. I hated coming home to an empty house. It was miserable and lonely. He defended it by saying he was making money for *us*. But if he rang, and I was out with Brett or some other friends, he'd get testy about it. He wanted the little woman at home waiting for him, and that simply wasn't my idea of bliss.'

'It sounds as though he might have been more considerate,' Natalie volunteered, wondering if Damien had enjoyed the company of *friends* while he was away.

'Considerate!' Lyn rolled her eyes. 'Most people are content to pay off a house over twenty or thirty years. Not Damien. He had his mind set on getting the house paid off as quickly as possible so we could start a family without any debts over our heads. We couldn't *waste* money on having a good time.'

A man who took his responsibilities seriously, Natalie thought, but that could be oppressive if taken too far. 'You never went out together?'

'Only when he could fit it into his schedule,' Lyn tossed off dismissively. 'It was nowhere near often enough for me. Life was boringly dull. Brett spent money as if there was a hole in the bucket. I hated being made accountable for what I spent out of our joint account.'

Natalie looked her surprise. 'I wouldn't have thought Damien was mean.'

Lyn heaved a sigh. 'I couldn't get him to understand that what I made myself simply wasn't sufficient for my needs. We married too early in life. Damien was pouring money into the business, trying to expand it. *Our future*, he called it. Brett was taking money out of the business on some loan arrangement so he could have a good time.'

'It sounds as if you should have married Brett,' Natalie said unhappily.

'You're right about that.'

And she should have married Damien, Natalie thought. *Both women had married the wrong man.* The thought hit Natalie forcefully. Perhaps it was something she had always recognised and sternly repressed in the hope that everything would eventually come right.

'Don't look so glum,' Lyn said with her infectious smile. 'Everything is going to turn out fine.'

'How do you know that?' Natalie couldn't help registering her surprise.

'Damien and I discussed you at some length, and the role you've played in his life.'

Natalie's instincts rose to the fore. There was something very wrong about this conversation, something she couldn't quite put her finger on yet...

'What conclusion did you come to?'

'You missed the boat, Natalie. Happily for me, I fell right into it.' She winked. 'It's called the rebound effect. Damien and I will very shortly be announcing our remarriage.'

Shock hammered through Natalie. It couldn't be true. Unless Damien had decided there would be no happiness with her, no matter how long he waited. She frantically searched her mind for something effective to say. Lyn sipped her brandy with a calm, self-satisfied serenity that left Natalie floundering.

'But...but...you said yourself you should have married Brett.'

Lyn put her glass on the table. The happy infectious smile spread wider. There was no bile in what she said. 'That was then. This is now. Damien can now afford me, and I'm now prepared to make him a father. The deal is done.'

She stood up and tucked her handbag under her arm. 'I wanted you to know,' she said with an air of confidentiality that was somehow insufferably smug. 'And by the way, I will do my best to give your career a boost. I hope it leads somewhere good for you.'

She sauntered off, not looking back, leaving Natalie to pay the bill.

CHAPTER ELEVEN

NATALIE seethed all the way home. Lyn Chandler had neatly sucked her in, drawn her out, dismissed the past, and moved in for the kill. She had obviously done the same thing to Damien, though with a different end in view.

Superficially Lyn was glittery gold, just like Brett, but underneath the bright patina was an unremitting core of self-centredness. If Damien thought his ex-wife had undergone a change of heart in regard to her priorities, he was sorely deluded. However, Lyn was undoubtedly clever enough to dress herself in tones that appealed to a man who had just been rejected, and holding out the carrot of having his child was a master stroke.

Lyn wouldn't be a good mother. Natalie was certain of it. Damien would end up being a parent, all right. Full-time. Either that, or hire a nanny. Natalie couldn't imagine Lyn taking kindly to changing nappies or losing sleep over a baby. As for the pampering she would demand throughout a pregnancy, the sky wouldn't even be the limit.

How could Damien be such a fool as to take that woman back into his life? Hadn't he learnt from his experience with her the first time around? Natalie was strongly tempted to go to his apartment and confront him with what he was inviting upon himself.

On the other hand, Damien was a highly intelligent man. Maybe he knew precisely what he was doing. Maybe he had already counted the cost of a second marriage to Lyn and accepted it as the price to be paid for the family he wanted. After all, Lyn had been his first choice as the mother of his children. His first love. Natalie couldn't be sure the *spark* wasn't still there. She had never seen Lyn and Damien together.

Of course, there was the possibility that Lyn was lying through her teeth about what had gone on with Damien last Saturday. When Lyn had poured out her woes over the break-up with Julian, Damien might have reciprocated with an account of the disastrous *fresh start* with Natalie. Perhaps, Lyn had seized the opportunity today to drive a decisive wedge into the situation between them, leaving the way open for her to inveigle Damien into a second marriage that would provide her with what she wanted.

In which case, she had to be stopped, and what better time than right now? Natalie no longer had any doubts about Damien's integrity. She was ready to make the commitment he wanted from her. She wanted to make it. She hoped she hadn't lost him through not trusting her instincts.

The taxi she had caught from the city pulled up at her house. Natalie didn't get out. She checked her watch. It was well past six o'clock. Damien would probably be home from work by now. If not, she could wait for him. She leaned forward and redirected the driver to Damien's apartment in Collaroy.

Natalie immediately started planning what she would say to Damien. The more she thought about it, the less she liked the various scenarios that ran through her mind. They all revolved around her visit to Lyn, and how could she explain that away without it being offensive to Damien?

'I went to find out what kind of husband you'd been.'

The scorn in his eyes would be spine-chilling. 'I see. Would you like to see my character references, as well?'

Worse was, 'I needed to know if you'd been unfaithful when you were married.'

Utter disgust. 'Still bracketing me with Brett.'

There was no way that Natalie could see where she could come out of it well. Her heart cramped as she imagined Damien saying, 'At least I know what to expect with Lyn. She won't be checking me out with all and sundry behind my back. Nor will she be flinging false and unfair accusations in my face.'

Natalie sagged back in the car-seat and closed her eyes. She had made a bed of nails for herself in not trusting Damien. How on earth was she going to climb out of it without lasting injury?

She remembered the words she had flung at him at Merlinmist... 'How can you ever be forgiven?' When she considered his patience, his caring, his unstinting giving to her, how could *she* ever be forgiven for accusing him of motives that related entirely to Brett?

'This is it, lady.'

Natalie's eyes flew open. She stared out at the block of apartments that contained the home Damien had made for himself. What was she going to do? What could she say?

'Want to change your mind again?' the driver asked cheerfully.

The memory of their parting at Merlinmist came rushing back to her... Damien's concern that he be told if she had conceived...a man who took his responsibilities seriously. She had put such an outcome to the back of her mind, not wanting to think about it or deal with it. But it was a way back to him, a far more effective way than trying to excuse her doubts and fears. If she *was* pregnant, delivering the news to Damien would give her the opportunity to demonstrate she now believed all he had told her.

Hopefully, it would also spike Lyn's guns!

'Driver, I need to go to a chemist shop. Do you know where there might be one open?'

'No problem,' he said, sounding amused.

Natalie flushed. He probably thought she was considering a 'hot date', and wanted to come prepared for all eventualities.

He drove straight to a shopping centre along one of the streets in Collaroy and parked outside a chemist's, engine and meter still running. Natalie rather unnecessarily asked him to wait. The driver was happily aware he was on easy money with this fare.

She purchased a pregnancy test-kit, enquiring of the pharmacist how long after conception would the test give a definitive result. He informed her that the tests were so sensitive now, it was possible to get a result within a couple of days. It would be accurate provided she followed the instructions accompanying the kit. Satisfied with this information, Natalie returned to the taxi.

'Back to the Narrabeen address, please, driver.'

'Whatever you like, lady,' he agreed, grinning from ear to ear.

Natalie felt considerably lighter-hearted herself. Of course, she might not be pregnant, but the test was, at least, a decisive place to start for formulating a plan to recover the ground she had lost with Damien.

Then a terrible thought struck her. If she had conceived last week . . . and if Damien had slept with Lyn on the rebound . . . and Lyn had deliberately missed taking whatever contraceptive pill she would probably have been using with

Julian... both of them could be pregnant to Damien. The thought of Damien becoming a father twice over at almost the same time made Natalie's hair rise.

It lent an extra urgency to using the test.

She could hardly make Damien's choice for him, but Natalie was not about to stand back and let Lyn make all the running where Damien was concerned. Certainly she could not afford to let a month go by before contacting him, pregnant or not. Somehow, she had to counteract the damage she had done in turning on him as she had at Merlinmist.

Once back at Narrabeen, Natalie paid off the taxi-driver, adding a tip that inspired him to wish her the best of luck. She would need every bit of it, she thought, wondering if Lyn was with Damien right at this moment, giving him *her* version of today's meeting, undermining Natalie's credibility with malice aforethought.

The instructions on the test-kit advised that early morning was the best time to carry out the test, when urine had been stored in the bladder for four hours.

Natalie spent a restless night. Damien's protests kept preying on her mind... 'Do I have to wait for another car accident? Another lifetime?'

She still had no recollection of the day of the accident. She suspected that Damien had revealed his desire for her and she had reacted badly, colouring his motives with Brett's attitudes. Had that come as a shock to him, finding himself put in another man's shoes?

Would she ever have accepted Damien's pursuit of her had she not lost her memory? Probably not. The emotional garbage from her marriage was mountainous. Only by having it cleared away for a while had she been able to see Damien in a different light. It was now paramount she convince him that the return of her memory would not form a running sore between them, a sore which would never heal.

Otherwise, Lyn *could* win.

It was with mixed feelings that Natalie carried out the test the next morning. It was wrong to use a child to hold a man. She couldn't... wouldn't do it. If Damien showed any sign of being unsure about their future together, she would not push for the marriage she now wanted. On the other hand, she could and would let him know where he stood with her.

The result was positive.

Relief and joy were swiftly followed by a sense of wonderment. She was going to have another child. Would it be a girl this time? It would be lovely to have a daughter, although of course a son would be just as welcome. The impulse to share the news with Damien had Natalie rushing to the telephone.

But telling him wasn't enough. She needed to be with him, to watch his face, to see how he responded to the confirmed fact of her having his child. That would tell her more than anything else how matters stood between them.

It was early. She had time to catch him at home before he went to work. Natalie dressed at top speed, rang for a taxi, and was on her way to Damien within twenty minutes. Again she spent the trip to his home planning what to say to him, how best to put it. She couldn't burst out with the simple fact she was pregnant. She needed to tell him much more. Or did she? Announcing their child-to-be might be the best ice-breaker.

Natalie was still in two minds about what approach to take as she stood outside Damien's door, waiting for him to answer the button she had pressed. She doubted she had ever felt quite so nervous in her life. Not even on the day she had married Brett.

The door opened.

Damien looked at her in blank surprise.

She stared back, choked by the memory of the intimacy she had rejected. He wasn't dressed. The short wrap-around robe he wore left a deep V of chest bare, as well as his forearms and lower legs. Whether he was completely naked underneath the robe or not was irrelevant. Natalie remembered him naked, and she was swept by a desire so strong that any words she might have spoken were completely jumbled in her mind. Her heart pumped a flood of heat through her body.

'Natalie?' The need to know what had brought her here sharpened Damien's eyes.

'I . . . I wanted to see you,' she said, struggling to regain some composure.

To her consternation, he didn't ask her in. An expression of tense reserve set on his face. He stepped outside the apartment, pulling the door almost shut behind him. It was such an unwelcoming stance, it froze Natalie into silence.

His body language was all wrong, stiff and offputting and reserved. Didn't he want her any more? Was he in a hurry to go somewhere? His hair was damp from a shower. She picked up the smell of his after-shave lotion, except it wasn't quite the same. It seemed to be mixed with some other scent. But she couldn't afford to be distracted by that. The important point was he obviously didn't want to give her much of his time. Which was a total turnaround from his attitude of last week.

'Is there some reason for coming to me at this early hour?' he asked.

The impulse to share the news of her pregnancy was shrivelled by his aloofness. 'I came back home yesterday,' she temporised. 'I was thinking of you. We . . . we didn't part very well.'

He grimaced. 'It was . . . difficult . . . for both of us. If you think I misled you after your accident . . .'

'No . . . no . . .' She shook her head vehemently. 'You were fair. If anyone's to blame for anything, it's me. I hope you don't think too badly of me.'

She searched his eyes anxiously. Had she lost him?

'What you asked was reasonable, Natalie,' he said flatly. 'I apologise for my outburst at the time. A month is not long, considering all that's gone before.'

'Maybe it doesn't have to be a month,' she suggested hopefully, trying her utmost to reach into his mind and heart. Surely he realised she did want him. She wouldn't have come otherwise.

The suggestion made him uneasy. 'I can wait.'

It was like a slap in the face. Was he giving her a taste of what she had dealt him? Was he savagely thinking, Let her wait, too?

She was seriously rattled by the distance he was keeping between them. 'Well, I guess I wanted to be sure of that,' she said slowly, letting him know she had not wiped him out of her life. If he wanted to know.

He nodded, not giving her any extra reassurance. It dawned on her that his nod was a dismissal. He wanted her to go. She stepped back, desperately wanting him to say something to stop her, to keep her with him.

He didn't.

'I wanted to know how you were,' she said.

'I'm fine.'

The brusque answer gave her no opening to go on with the conversation. She nodded. Too many times. Feeling hopelessly foolish, she dropped her gaze to his bare chest. She wondered whether or not it would break the dreadful barrier he had slid between them if she reached out and touched him. She couldn't find the courage to do it.

The thought came to Natalie that he didn't trust her any more. She had acted on impulse in directing him to Merlinmist. He probably thought this early morning visit was another impulse that could all too easily go wrong.

We're going to have a baby, her heart cried, but it was impossible to tell him under these circumstances. Pregnancy could feel like a trap. She had known that feeling once. She couldn't give it to someone else. Maybe Damien had endured enough of her. He might even now be balancing what he felt for her against what Lyn offered him.

Natalie could not bring herself to throw their unborn child onto the scales. It was wrong. Terribly wrong. She was mad to have thought of it.

'I'm sorry for interrupting your dressing,' she said stiffly, chilled by the paucity of his response to her. 'I'll go now.'

'I hope you have a pleasant day,' he said with formal politeness.

'You, too,' she returned, then hurried away from him, miserably embarrassed by the whole scene.

She could feel Damien's eyes burning into her back. She wondered, if she turned quickly, would she see the blaze of desire she desperately wanted to see? No, he wanted her to go. He was watching her go.

She went. She walked straight past the elevator and took the staircase. It wasn't a month any more, she reminded herself. Only another three weeks. The hurt would stop then. On both sides. It had to. She couldn't bear to contemplate anything else.

CHAPTER TWELVE

ON HER return home from the disturbing visit to Damien, Natalie settled in front of her computer, needing to take grasp of some purpose in her life, telling herself she had work to do. It would make the time go faster if she immersed herself in her work.

Concentration eluded her. She sat blankly in front of the monitor screen, unable to summon the necessary will-power to actually strike a key. Her mind kept revolving around the consequences of the decisions she had made. Especially Damien's reaction to her this morning.

The ringing of the door-chimes was a welcome distraction, providing relief, however short, from her tormenting thoughts. She didn't wonder who was calling on her. She was simply grateful for some activity.

Damien stood on her porch.

He was dressed in a business suit, ready for work, but his eyes seared hers with questions. Natalie's breath caught in her throat, rendering her speechless. Her eyes clung to his, pleading for a change of heart from his earlier standoffishness.

'Do you want me, Natalie?'

'Yes.' She expelled the word on a rush of breath that emptied her lungs.

'Certain?'

She nodded.

'Is it right for you now?'

A huge well of emotion threatened to choke her again. 'Yes.' It was a bare whisper.

Whatever uncertainties had plagued Damien's mind were summarily dismissed. He stepped forward and swept her into his arms. There was no more talking, no more thinking, no more agonising. He kissed her, and there was no holding back from Natalie. She responded with all the pent-up feeling that had been gathering force since they had shared the bed at Merlinmist.

She craved the warm solidity of him, the passion of his desire for her. She needed to feel it was real, substantial, so deeply connected to her that it could never be taken by any other woman. 'Love me,' she pleaded. 'Love me as I've never been loved before, Damien.'

The front door was shut. He scooped her off her feet and carried her into the master bedroom. She didn't care that it was the bed she had previously shared with Brett. Damien superseded everything she had known with her former husband. He was earth and fire and air and water to her. He was life.

Clothes were discarded in wild haste. There was no sense of discovery this time, only a driving need to have and to hold, to lose all doubts and fears in the ecstatic security of coming together, being as one, their bodies the perfect instruments to bring harmony from the discord generated by the recovery of her memory.

Natalie had never really experienced lust before, yet from the moment she convulsed in sheer bliss around Damien she was gripped by a wild, insatiable greed to know and exult in every pleasure their bodies could find and indulge in. It was as though every fantasy she'd ever had about Damien as a lover sprang to life in her mind, demanding expression and absolute fulfilment ... the power, the passion, the sensuality, the stamina, the intense virility of the man unleashed, coursing from his body to hers in tidal waves of sensation.

She wallowed in his lust for her, floated in it, drowned in it, incited it with a wantonness she had not known herself capable of. Perhaps it was inspired by the release of a host of repressions built up over years. Or the fear that she might have squandered the chance to take and know and feel all that Damien was.

Whether he sensed this rampaging compulsion within her and responded to it, or whether he was sating his own frustrated needs and desires, Natalie had no idea. Their feelings melded in a long, tempestous lovemaking that was intensely mutual, intensely satisfying, and overwhelmingly different from anything she had known with Brett.

Only exhaustion tamed their ardour for each other, and even when their energy was totally depleted, the need to touch, in however a desultory fashion, kept them enthralled with each other. She loved the feel of his firm muscles, the tight smoothness of his skin. She caught a faint scent of his aftershave lotion. Not the one she had smelled earlier. He must have disliked that and washed it off in favour of this one. Natalie liked it better, too. It was enticingly sexy, just like Damien.

Natalie couldn't help thinking back over her marriage to Brett, how devoid it had been of this kind of togetherness. Her mind inevitably drifted to Damien's marriage. Had it been this good for him with Lyn? This...*complete*?

She shied from the idea, but it kept nagging, fraying the edges of her contentment. Damien had been with Lyn on Saturday night. There would have been no grounds for Lyn's words and actions yesterday if there had been no meeting between them. Had Damien succumbed to a rebound effect? Was that why he had been so distant this morning, feeling it wasn't right to resume a relationship with her?

Yet he had come after her.

'Was the sex in your marriage good, Damien?' she asked.

'I thought it was.' His voice was rich with contentment as he added, 'You've revolutionised my thoughts.'

She smiled, happy that he was happy. All the same, she would be happier still to have the matter of Lyn completely cleared away. She couldn't help dreading the thought of what might have happened on Saturday night.

'Did you ever sleep with your ex-wife after your marriage ended?'

'Yes.'

Natalie fought against tensing up. What was done was done. It would be different after this morning.

'I had the crazy idea I could win her back,' Damien went on in a light, self-mocking tone. 'It was soon after the divorce. Lyn indulged me. She liked the power.'

Relief poured through Natalie. She had nothing to worry about. Damien was talking about years ago. Before they'd ever met. Yet his words stirred her curiosity about the woman who'd caused her so much concern.

'You mean she used you to boost her ego?'

'Something like that,' he said carelessly. 'She relished having me run after her, but had no intention of meeting me halfway. Once I realised that, I let go.' His fingers trailed down the curve of her spine. 'It's not easy to accept failure when you've been fully committed. Is that why you never showed you knew about Brett's infidelities, Natalie?'

'Pride,' she answered. 'We had a lot of arguments about it. He'd promise me . . .' She sighed.

'If it hadn't been for Ryan...but it doesn't matter now.'

She thought of the baby she had conceived, their child, Damien's and hers, then decided there were other things she wanted to tell Damien first, the feelings she had denied for most of the years they had known each other.

'I used to wonder how it might be with you,' she confessed, luxuriating in the freedom from all inhibitions.

Damien pressed a kiss on her forehead. 'You remember actually thinking that?'

'Yes. Sometimes it hurt to watch you with other women. I hated feeling so...affected by you.'

'You hid it extremely well,' he said with a dry touch of irony.

She hitched herself up, wanting him to see the truth in her eyes. 'I saw you as being like Brett. I know that's not true, Damien, and never was. I think it was some kind of defence to shut off the feelings you stirred. I was ashamed of having them. I blamed you for things I had no right to blame you for, because it helped me to push away thoughts I didn't want to have.'

'There was always a current of attraction between us, Natalie. You buried it so deep I began to despair of your ever acknowledging it. I did not think you could ever be mine.'

'I acknowledge it now. It was there all the time. That polarity. That pull.'

He smiled. His eyes glinted deep satisfaction. 'I think we just proved that.' The smile widened. 'Of course, we could try improving the proof.'

She laughed and rolled on to her back, stretching her body provocatively. 'I'm a limp rag,' she declared, her eyes teasing. 'The energy will have to come from you.'

'I've suddenly discovered vast reserves of it.'

As he was poising his body to demonstrate his rejuvenation, the telephone rang. Damien did not so much as glance at the handset on the bedside table. Natalie was very much inclined to ignore it, as well. She held her breath and focused all her concentration on feeling the marvellous sensation of Damien entering her once again. He did it very slowly, with a sensual roll that was exquisitely exciting.

The telephone stopped ringing.

Natalie sighed with ecstatic pleasure as she felt Damien's full length pushed past the edge of her womb.

The telephone nagged again with a persistent buzzing.

'It might be important,' Damien said with a wicked twinkle in his eyes. 'I think you should answer it.' Holding himself deep within her, he reached out, picked up the receiver, and handed it to her. Then he continued moving them both in a highly erotic rhythm.

'... Kippax.'

The name spoken from the receiver filtered through the delicious bombardment of tingling sensations, snapping Natalie's mind into some alertness.

'Sharon! Help. I mean, hello,' she managed somewhat breathlessly.

'I'm glad you're home.' The friendly voice was warm with relief. 'I've called a few times, but no answer. I was beginning to worry about you. What have you been up to?'

'Many things,' she gasped. Damien was building a momentum that was far too distracting for her to put two thoughts together. 'Stop it!' she hissed. 'It's my editor!'

'Tell her you're receiving inspiration.'

He was an absolute devil but she loved him. She loved what he was doing to her, too. She took a deep breath and tried to be sane.

'I had a few days away,' she explained to Sharon. 'There's no problem with my memory now. I'm about to get back to work.'

'You are at work,' Damien muttered. He was really moving quickly now. She hoped the bed wouldn't start squeaking.

'That's wonderful! I might have another commission for you if you're interested.'

'How exciting!'

'This is just the preliminaries,' Damien promised, his eyes laughing as she squirmed around him.

'Is there any chance of you coming in to my office this morning?' Sharon asked.

'I'll find out.' She put her hand over the receiver. 'Is there any chance of my meeting my editor this morning?' she whispered urgently.

'Possibly...possibly...' He was getting too worked up to concentrate properly.

'Possibly,' Natalie answered.

'I have the manuscript here,' Sharon pressed. 'Another children's book. I'd like to discuss it with you.'

Excitement was swelling through her in waves. Both of them must climax soon. 'Would an hour...from now...be all right? I'll be able...to come then.'

'I expect you to come before then,' Damien put in purposefully.

'Great! Bye for now.'

'Thanks, Sharon.'

Impossible to replace the receiver. It fell from Natalie's hand as she succumbed to the pleasures of the moment, riding a crest of sweet exultation until Damien had delivered all he had promised.

Afterwards they showered together, which was a splendid way to extend the glorious intimacy they had shared.

Damien offered to drive her to the publisher's offices and took a great deal of pleasure in watching her dress for her meeting with Sharon. Once they were on their way, it occurred to

Natalie that they hadn't made any arrangement for getting together again.

'Will I see you later today?' she asked, aware he was dressed for business, as well.

'I think I should take you out to dinner tonight. We mightn't eat otherwise.' The glint of lust in his eyes was an intoxicant in itself. 'Would you be ready by seven-thirty?'

She laughed. 'With bells on.'

There wasn't time to tell him about their child now. But tonight... Natalie wanted to hug herself, her happiness soaring beyond anything she'd ever known... Tonight was going to be the best night of her life!

CHAPTER THIRTEEN

NATALIE breezed into the building that housed her publishing company. She felt on top of the world and full of zest for the prospect of taking on a new creative project. It was only when she stepped out of the elevator on Sharon's floor that her buoyant spirits suffered a slight puncture.

This was where she had seen the woman in the yellow suit. Natalie frowned. She was sure she had recognised that woman. The image of her wearing black was very strong. It vexed Natalie that she couldn't place her. She had the feeling it was not a happy association. Which probably meant that the woman had been one of Brett's side interests.

Natalie brushed aside the cynical thought. It was hardly reasonable anyway. How would Brett get to meet a high-powered lady in the publishing world? Natalie had certainly not introduced her to him. She'd had no connection to this publishing company until well after Brett's death.

There had to be some other answer.

She announced her appointment with Sharon to the receptionist and was waved on with a nod and a smile. Sharon eagerly welcomed her, and they very quickly got down to business. The story submitted by the author was a fantasy adventure, set on a fictional planet far from Earth. The description of its inhabitants and their environment allowed Natalie a great deal of creative licence and her imagination caught fire with what could be done.

Sharon specified the number of colour plates she wanted for the book. She also wanted the cover design to extend over the front and back of the hardcover edition, and be intriguing as well as spectacular. She had the feeling this book could become a big seller.

Satisfied that Natalie's ideas for illustrations would enhance the story, Sharon had no hesitation in moving on to discussing a new contract.

'I expect you'll be wanting better terms on this book.'

Natalie grinned. 'I won't say no.'

'I'll bring up some figures on the computer.'

Natalie watched Sharon's fingers fly over the keyboard. Information flashed up on the monitor screen. It was amazing how much could be stored and so easily retrieved on a computer.

The thought struck her that computers had been Brett's business. Computers were everywhere these days. A publishing company might have very specific needs that were not answered by general purpose software.

'Did this company ever hire anyone to do a computer conversion?' she asked.

Sharon looked surprised. 'Yes, they did. Everything runs beautifully now.'

Natalie's mouth went dry. 'How long ago?'

'It was being completed when I first started here. A couple of years ago.'

'Do you remember the people who did the conversion?'

Sharon's bright hazel eyes sparkled. 'Do I? Two of the most gorgeous hunks I've ever seen. Not that *I* got an introduction. They dealt strictly at the executive level.'

'What was the company name?'

'CCS.'

Damien and Brett. And Anne Smith was executive level. There *was* a connection.

'Is something wrong?'

'No, there's nothing wrong.' Natalie tried to smile, but the floodgates on her last missing recollections were swinging open.

The woman in black.

Black.

The memory slammed into Natalie's mind with heart-stopping force.

The funeral!

Anne Smith was the woman who hadn't stopped weeping, the woman Damien had had no time for, although he should have if their story had been true.

Natalie remembered now. All of it. Ryan and Brett and Anne Smith at the top of the cliff, Damien abseiling down the face of it. Anne

Smith...the only witness to what had happened...how Ryan had come to fall...how Brett had failed to stop him from going too close to the edge.

She had said Ryan had chased after a ball. But what had she and Brett been doing in those few critical moments it took for Ryan to run out of reach?

The explanation had never rung true to Natalie. She had brought Ryan up to be careful. He had not been the kind of child who would run heedlessly into mortal danger. Despite his love of playing with balls, he wouldn't follow one over a cliff. He would call out to Daddy to get it back for him.

'Natalie? Are you all right?'

The question roused her out of the dark introspection. She refocused her eyes on Sharon.

'You've gone as pale as a ghost,' Sharon observed in concern.

The ghosts were gathering with a vengeance.

'Just a bit faint,' Natalie excused. 'I was so busy rushing around this morning I didn't have time for breakfast.'

'Sorry. I should have offered you a coffee. How do you like it? Milk and sugar?'

'Yes, please. One sugar.'

'I'll get one for you now. And bring some biscuits, as well.'

'Thank you.'

Sharon quickly rose from her chair and left the office to fetch the offered sustenance. Natalie was relieved to be left to her thoughts. They were too painful and private to share with anyone, and too pressingly urgent to put aside.

Anne Smith. Sharon's boss, who had ordered Sharon to handle Natalie Hayes by herself. It was sheer accident that Natalie had seen her here. Otherwise they would never have met in this building.

It amazed Natalie that the woman had risked giving her a job at all, regardless of talent. Apart from any unpleasantness that might rise out of the situation, surely the woman wouldn't want to have any reminder of a tragedy in which she had been involved? Particularly if she was guilty of negligence. Or worse.

On the other hand, guilt could lead to remorse, to the urge to compensate. Natalie remembered Sharon saying that Anne Smith had taken one look at the work Natalie had submitted—or the name attached to that work—and ordered that she be put under contract to the company. Ryan was gone forever, but perhaps a job might help the bereaved mother—was that how her mind had reasoned?

Or did pride in her position as project manager take first place? Perhaps her executive status demanded the attitude that talent was talent, no matter who, what or where. Certainly Sharon was impressed with Natalie's work.

Natalie felt a burning need to know the truth of what had happened. But would it serve any good purpose to pursue the past when she had so much to look forward to in the future? Did she really want to stir up again all the pain surrounding Ryan's death? She couldn't bring her beloved son back. She was going to have another child.

Her thoughts shifted to Damien. She had given him her trust. It would be wrong to start doubting him now. He had sworn that Anne Smith had been with him that weekend, not Brett, and Natalie believed him. Nevertheless, Anne Smith had known both men. She might have accompanied Damien on the trip, but was it Damien she had wanted?

Had Damien believed Anne Smith's account of events on the clifftop? Did he have any doubts himself? He had said to her that accidents like that happened so quickly. What made him so sure, particularly when he hadn't been right there to see with his own eyes?

And Anne Smith...what of her? Could she be believed?

Sharon returned with the coffee and a plate of shortbread biscuits. Natalie made the effort to eat one between sips of coffee. Sharon discussed what terms she was prepared to offer on the contract. The thought of Anne Smith simmered in the back of Natalie's mind. She came to an agreement with Sharon but had no idea what it was. She simply accepted the proposals put to her. Sharon promised to have the typed contract in the mail to Natalie by tomorrow.

'That's it, then,' Sharon said with satisfaction.

'I guess it is,' Natalie said heavily.

'Let me show you out.'

'No. I'll be all right,' Natalie assured her. She knew what she was going to do and she didn't want Sharon at her side.

Her meeting with Anne Smith would not touch on editorial responsibilities.

She smiled as she stood up to take her leave. 'Thank you for looking after me. I'll deliver the best work I can.'

'I'm sure you will.'

They parted on that mutual note of goodwill, and Natalie walked back along the corridor to the receptionist's desk.

She expected to be fobbed off. Anne Smith clearly didn't want any contact with her. Natalie was determined to force it, one way or another. She had a right to know how and why Ryan had died.

'I wish to see Miss Smith,' she said with steely resolution.

The receptionist gave an aplogetic smile. 'Miss Smith has a very busy schedule. You would need to make an appointment to see her. Would you like me to call her secretary?'

'I want Miss Smith informed directly, right now, immediately, that Mrs Hayes is here to see her. The matter will not wait. It concerns her dead child.'

The receptionist's eyes widened in surprise and shock. 'Very well,' she assented.

Regardless of how busy Anne Smith's schedule was, the reaction was swift and decisive. A secretary came to collect Natalie. A few minutes later she was ushered into the project manager's office.

Anne Smith was standing behind her desk. She made no move to come forward to greet Natalie. The two women eyed each other as antagonists with much of personal value lying between them. Natalie took grim satisfaction from the little signs of strain showing on the other woman's beautiful face: the tightness around her mouth, the wariness in her eyes, the sharp tilt of her chin.

She was wearing a vibrant green suit today, a bright lime-green that accentuated her dark colouring. But Natalie remembered her in black far too well to be impressed or influenced by the other woman's power dressing.

'How can I help you, Mrs Hayes?' The polite question was accompanied by a gestured invitation for Natalie to take a chair.

'I want to know the truth about my son's death,' Natalie stated bluntly, not prepared to sit while the other woman remained standing.

'I said all I had to say at the inquest. I have nothing to add. I'm sorry...'

'You lied.'

Anne Smith raised her finely arched eyebrows. 'That is a very serious allegation.'

'Who retrieved the ball that was supposed to have rolled over the cliff?'

Two hot spots appeared high on her cheeks. 'I didn't know it was retrieved.'

'Don't you consider it strange that it was in Ryan's bag when the police returned it to me?'

'I don't understand...'

'I know you're lying.'

'Perhaps we should leave the conversation there, Mrs Hayes. Knowing and proving are two different things.'

'You could face perjury charges, Miss Smith,' Natalie fired at her, hoping to crack her defences.

The beautiful dark eyes flashed defiance. 'Then I'll face them if I have to, and pay what penalties need to be paid...if I have to.'

'You could go to gaol.'

Her eyes narrowed, calculating the risk. 'And you might never realise how lucky you are,' she said with slow deliberation. 'You have Damien Chandler as a...friend. You might lose him...forever.'

'Tell me the truth, Miss Smith.'

'I can't.'

'What happened on the top of that cliff?'

'Only one person can tell you that.'
'And you're the one.'
'No.'
'Who then?'
'Damien Chandler.'

CHAPTER FOURTEEN

IT HAD proved impossible to draw anything further from Anne Smith on the subject. Natalie was deeply disturbed by her insistence that only Damien could tell her the truth about Ryan's death. It left her with the inference that Damien had hidden from her the truth of where he was at the time of the accident.

It might not be a case of covering up for Brett. Perhaps Damien had been at fault in some way. Perhaps it was Anne Smith's fault. Perhaps they were all at fault, and the agreement had been made that the memories of the dead should wait upon the realities of the living.

Natalie recoiled from that idea. She didn't want Damien to be involved in any circumstances that had led directly to her son's death. Besides, it couldn't be true. Anne Smith had expressed the opinion that Natalie was lucky to have Damien as a friend. It was a very supportive statement on his behalf. She must have had good reason to give it.

Not that Natalie needed to be told by Anne Smith how good a friend Damien had been to her. She was well aware of that herself. He was the most wonderful lover she could ever have. No way was she going to jeopardise her future with Damien. There had to be a reasonable explanation for the course of action he'd decided upon concerning that fateful weekend.

Despite telling herself this, over and over again, Natalie still couldn't let the matter go. She wanted it cleared up, once and for all. Then she could let it rest in peace and concentrate entirely on the future.

The thought of bringing the subject up at dinner was less than appealing. She no longer felt in the mood to dress up and celebrate the end of all that had kept her apart from Damien. She needed to talk to him about Ryan.

Since Damien was to be at her house at seven-thirty, Natalie decided he would probably be home from work by six o'clock. It was no longer of any concern to her if they went out to dinner at all. She felt too unsettled to wait until seven-thirty to see him.

It was six-fifteen when she pressed the bell-button at his apartment. Natalie was not kept in suspense. The door was opened within a few moments. Damien looked startled to see her, naturally enough considering the arrangement they had made. He was clearly in the midst of changing his clothes since he wore the wrap-around robe he had greeted her in this morning.

'I had to come, Damien,' Natalie rushed out apologetically.

'Is there a problem?' he asked, a frown of concern creasing his brows together.

She was momentarily distracted by a waft of the same scent she'd smelled this morning. It struck her as odd because his jaw wasn't freshly shaven. She pushed the irrelevant thought aside and concentrated on what was important.

'May I come in?'

He hesitated, his frown deepening.

A voice floated from his living-room.

'Shall I fix you a drink, darling?'

Lyn's voice!

Another recognition speared into Natalie's mind, shattering in its implications. It was Lyn's perfume she could smell on Damien. It had come from him this morning while he kept her out of his apartment. And now...after he had been with her!

Natalie's heart froze. Her skin chilled. She looked at Damien with wounded eyes. 'Couldn't you wait a month for me?' she cried, stricken to her soul that she had given herself to him so completely while he...what had he been doing? Satisfying a long-frustrated lust for her?

His face tightened. His hand lifted towards her.

Natalie backed away, turned, and ran to the elevator, slamming her hand on the down button.

The doors slid open, the compartment not having moved since she'd stepped out of it.

'Natalie...'

Damien's call rang in her ears, harsh and commanding. She whirled forward and hit the button for the ground floor, desperate to escape the situation. She couldn't bear to expose her feelings under Lyn's gloating eyes. She didn't want to hear Damien's justification for his duplicity. Perhaps it was her fault he had turned to Lyn, but that couldn't excuse tonight. Not after their lovemaking this morning.

Damien beat the closing of the doors. He slammed his hand on the button to keep them held open, then confronted her, chest heaving, eyes blazing with anger.

'Be damned if I'll stand still for any more of your false assumptions about me, Natalie!' he thundered at her. 'I am *not* Brett. The woman in my apartment is my ex-wife. She calls all men *darling*. It's typical of the crowd she mixes with.'

Tears of confusion and bewilderment welled into Natalie's eyes. 'But she...you...'

'Come back and meet her for yourself.'

It finally penetrated the emotional chaos seizing Natalie's mind that Damien's anger was the anger of an innocent man who had been placed in a compromising position. When he lost patience with her dumbstruck stare, he took her hand and pulled her with him, determined that this particular contretemps be resolved right here and now.

Natalie followed numbly, her stomach churning, her head sickeningly awhirl with what might eventuate with Lyn. Damien closed the door to his apartment behind them and ushered Natalie into the living-room where her feet faltered to a wary halt.

Lyn was seated on one of the stools at the bar, sipping a martini, looking very much at home. Her only garment appeared to be an oversized T-shirt, probably belonging to Damien. Her hair was ruffled as though she'd just got out of bed. She gave Natalie one of her deeply dimpled smiles. Natalie's facial muscles were too stiff to return it. Although she wouldn't have returned that smile even if she could.

Damien moved forward to bridge the gap between the two women. He started an introduction. 'Natalie, this is Lyn...'

'We met yesterday,' Lyn cut in brightly, putting down her glass and sliding off the stool with mesmerising confidence. She stretched with the sinuous grace of a dangerous cat, ensuring the soft fabric of the T-shirt outlined every naked curve beneath it. Her nipples pouted from seemingly perfect breasts and she rolled her hips as though loosening up tired muscles.

Damien frowned at his ex-wife. 'You didn't tell me about any meeting.'

Lyn shrugged and undulated towards him, her hands lifted in appeal. 'It wasn't good news, darling. I think the only positive thing Natalie said about you was that you weren't mean with money. Now I, on the other hand...' she insinuated her arm around Damien's, cuddling up to him '...extolled all your virtues. And I do appreciate them, Damien. I really do.'

The feline purr made Natalie's hackles rise.

Damien coldly extracted himself from her kittenish hold. 'I don't know what game you think you're playing, Lyn, but I don't appreciate it one bit. Tell Natalie why you're here.'

Lyn was unperturbed. 'Natalie knows I've broken up with Julian, darling. And I told her I came to you. She's well aware of the situation. There's no need to get stuffy about it. She understands.'

Damien's gaze swung to Natalie, piercingly sharp. 'What do you understand, Natalie?'

Lyn had lied to her. Damien had lied by omission, not telling her Lyn was staying with him. But perhaps he had good reason for that. One thing was patently clear to Natalie. There was no intimacy here. Absolutely none from Damien. Lyn's performance *was* a performance. It didn't gell with Damien's reactions.

'Your ex-wife told me you and she would shortly be announcing your remarriage,' she answered flatly.

'Not a chance in hell!' His response was so peremptory and decisive, there was no doubting it. Damien looked grim. 'Is that why you asked about her this morning, Natalie?'

'Yes.'

'But you didn't believe me.' His eyes seethed with resentment.

'I did believe you, Damien,' Natalie asserted. 'I'm sorry for doubting you just now, but when I heard her voice and smelled her perfume on you...'

'She drowned my robe in it. Spilled the damned stuff all over it. I haven't had time to get it laundered.' He turned a look of icy contempt to the woman beside him. 'You're a bitch, Lyn. An out-and-out bitch.'

'Why? Because I've got the guts to go after what I want?' She tossed her head in defiant pride. 'It was good for us once, Damien. It could be good for us again.'

'That time is well and truly gone, and you know it, Lyn.'

She flicked a sly look at Natalie. 'You let me stay here with you.'

'I felt sorry for you.' His mouth twisted self-mockingly. 'Wasted sympathy. You'll always bite the hand that feeds you.'

'You're wrong, Damien. I'll give you what you want...'

'I don't want it from you. I stopped wanting it from you a long time ago.'

'I'll give you a baby...'

'No damned way!'

She nodded towards Natalie. 'What if she won't have you? I'd give you more than one baby. I'm ready to give you the family you want, Damien.'

A muscle in his jaw contracted. 'Go and get dressed, Lyn. I want you out of my life. Now. And don't ever come back to me again. Not for anything.'

'You're a fool, Damien. If you'll...'

'Move *now*,' he commanded tersely. 'Either that or I'll gather your belongings and you can dress in the lobby outside.'

She shot Natalie a venomous look as she flounced away from Damien and headed off to the hallway leading to the rest of the apartment. She left a silence bristling with tension. Not until a door slammed shut behind her did Damien turn to Natalie. His eyes were hard and glittering with challenge.

'Lyn came here on Saturday night,' he stated flatly. 'She'd had a violent fight with her lover. There were bruises on her upper arms. She asked if she could stay until she found an apartment for herself. She slept in the study if you want to check.'

'I believe you, Damien,' Natalie said quietly.

His mouth thinned. He shook his head. 'Lyn set this up so you would come and catch me with her. And you came.'

'No. It didn't enter my mind she'd be here with you. I came this morning because . . .' She didn't want to tell him she was pregnant while Lyn was still here. Her eyes pleaded for his understanding. 'I had a bad night. I realised, after the meeting with Lyn yesterday, how blind and foolish I'd been in misjudging you. And how very much I wanted to keep you in my life.'

He searched her eyes for several nerve-racking moments. 'I didn't know why you'd come. You said a month. And Lyn was here. I thought you'd think the worst . . .'

'As I did just now.' She made an apologetic gesture.

He shook his head. 'It was stupid of me to open my mouth to Lyn about you. It was a way of letting her know she couldn't use me for consolation. I had no idea . . .'

'I know,' Natalie broke in gently. 'There's no need to explain. If I'd stayed with you, none of this would have happened.'

'Why did you come here tonight, Natalie? After what we shared this morning, did you still feel driven to check up on me?'

His eyes burned with a need so intense it shamed Natalie for all she had put him through.

'Please forgive me for doubting you, Damien.' Her feet moved of their own accord, impelled to go to him. 'I swear I didn't come to check on you. It never occurred to me that Lyn would be here. She wasn't on my mind at all.' She lifted her hands to his chest, her eyes begging his belief. 'And I don't link you with Brett. Not any more.'

Damien caught her hands and held them still, his eyes deeply pained as he said, 'There has to be trust, Natalie.'

'On both sides,' she reminded him. 'If you'd told me Lyn was staying with you...'

'Yes, I realise that. I...' He heaved a deep sigh. 'When does it end...this feeling that I have to keep fighting what Brett did to you?'

A door slammed again, fracturing the false sense of being alone together. Lyn reappeared, shooting them a look of haughty scorn. 'How touching!'

'Goodbye, Lyn,' Damien said curtly.

She paused on her way to the front door, a malicious little smile curving her lips. 'I had Brett, too. He was a more exciting lover than you, Damien.' Her green eyes stabbed briefly at Natalie. 'You just can't get it right, can you?' she said pityingly.

'Witch!' Natalie retaliated in anger.

'Bitch!' Damien flung at his ex-wife.

Lyn didn't wait for any more. Having put them both down as best she could, she made her exit with another slam.

Natalie felt acutely discomfited by this further revelation of infidelity, and the crude comparison between Brett and Damien. 'It's not true, Damien,' she said, flushing at the need to say it.

'Typical of Lyn, wanting to twist the knife. Another lie,' he said with a snort of disgust. 'Brett never touched her.'

'How do you know?'

'He told me so after Lyn and I had parted. He said she'd made a play for him and he swore he hadn't taken her up on it. He told me because he didn't want her making any trouble between us out of spite.'

'And you believed him?'

'Yes. Brett wouldn't have risked our relationship. Not for an idle screw. And that's all it would have been to him.'

'Yet he risked his relationship with me. Over and over again,' she said with a pang of hurt. 'You meant more to him than I did.'

'Natalie...' He winced. 'Brett needed me. He needed you. Despite the way he used sex as a cover for his inadequacies and feelings of worthlessness, you were *his* woman, the only one who really counted.'

She had come to realise that, although it hadn't given her any satisfaction. But for Ryan, she would have walked away from Brett and nothing in the world could have talked her back into being his wife.

'Yet I came to despise him for the way he kept playing around behind your back,' Damien continued. 'I wanted to take you away from him, Natalie. I wanted you so damned much...'

His lips suddenly clamped shut over the words that had been spilling from them. He made a visible effort to relax his face into a lighter expression. His mouth tilted into a rueful smile.

'Why am I talking about the past when it's the last thing I want to do? That's all over.'

'Not quite, Damien.'

She hesitated, wondering if she should simply let sleeping dogs lie. Was the compulsion to know what had happened a destructive one? Yet didn't trust only come with truth? If Damien had told her Lyn was with him... if she had told Damien she'd seen Lyn yesterday... It was what was left unsaid that preyed on the mind, providing fertile ground for doubts and misunderstandings.

'I saw Anne Smith today,' she blurted out, wanting it over quickly. 'I asked her what happened on top of the cliff. Before Ryan fell. I never believed the story about the ball, Damien.'

He closed his eyes as though wanting to block out the memory of it. 'What did she say?' His voice was completely toneless.

'She said to ask you. That only you could tell me the truth.'

He dropped her hands and walked over to the windows overlooking the ocean. He stared out to sea, his shoulders slumping for several moments, as though the secret burden he carried was too heavy to bear. Then his back stiffened and he turned around. The bleak look of desperation on his face squeezed her heart with fear.

'I lied to you about that day, Natalie. I did cover up for Brett. And for you. To save you from unnecessary pain. But it was not so much Brett's fault that Ryan died. It was mine.'

CHAPTER FIFTEEN

'No.' THE word welled up from deeply instinctive knowledge and burst from Natalie's lips. She shook her head in absolute denial of Damien's claim of guilt. 'You wouldn't have done anything to hurt a little boy. You wouldn't have done anything to hurt Ryan. I don't believe it.'

There was an agony of desperate desire in his eyes. 'I was thinking of you. I never once considered the effect on Ryan. I wanted the whole unbearable charade to come to an end.'

'You...me...Brett...my marriage to him. You wanted it to end?'

'Yes.' It was an explosive hiss of emotion. 'Apart from your wedding night, and I couldn't believe it of him then, I never covered up for Brett's infidelities, Natalie. I wanted you to find him out. I wanted you to leave him. I wanted you to turn to me.'

'But...you were Brett's only friend.'

'He didn't love you. He didn't deserve you.' Damien smashed his fist into his other palm. 'I felt like killing him every time he talked of having had some other woman. It killed me that you seemed oblivious to it all. That if you knew of

174

it, you tolerated it, while my own love for you had to remain secluded, hidden and unfulfilled.'

'I would never have told you, Damien. What happens within a marriage is private.'

'Private!' He made the word sound like torture. 'It was a public humiliation, a public joke. It ended up feeling like an albatross around my neck. I couldn't come to you. Without breaching trust...honour...loyalty...call it what you will...I couldn't do it. The only chance for us, Natalie, was for you to turn to me.' His eyes glittered his determination. 'So I set out to make that happen.'

'You wouldn't have meant any harm,' she defended him.

'Yes, I did. Not to Ryan. To Brett.'

'It would never have turned out that way. I couldn't turn to you. Not then.'

Natalie knew it would never have happened. To her way of thinking then, Damien had been no better than Brett. She'd despised the effect Damien had on her. She would have told herself that turning to Damien would have been akin to leaping out of the frying-pan into the fire. But Damien hadn't known that.

'I knew Brett wanted Anne Smith,' he went on remorselessly. 'All the more so because she had refused him. That didn't happen very often with Brett.'

No, Natalie thought with bitter cynicism. Brett had had the looks and the body to turn most women on. If all they'd wanted was to know what it was like with him, Brett wouldn't have left them in doubt.

'I thought a weekend in close proximity would present an irresistible challenge to him. He'd try again, and I'd make damned sure you saw it. I imagined taking you into my arms... comforting you... making you realise...' His hands lifted and fell in a contorted gesture of anguished appeal.

'But I didn't go,' Natalie said flatly, all too heart-chillingly aware of why she hadn't gone.

He shook his head as though his thoughts were too painful to dwell on. 'I was counting on it so much... so much...'

He walked over to a sofa, paused, picked up a cushion, looked down at it, plucked at its roulade edging. 'When Brett turned up at the camping site, there was only Ryan with him. You weren't the only one who was sick, Natalie. I was so sick with disappointment, I wasn't fair to Anne.'

He raised eyes that had emptied of all expression. 'I liked her as a person. She was bright, easy company. I'd dated her a few times. But that weekend I didn't give her the attention she had every right to expect. Nor could I give her what she wanted from me.'

'You didn't try to make love to her,' Natalie supplied quietly.

He tossed the cushion aside, commenced walking towards her. 'I offered only company.' His mouth twisted savagely. 'Not very good company. I paid more attention to Ryan. At least he was part of you.'

Yes, very much part of me, Natalie thought on a wave of desolation for how much she had lost when Ryan's life had been cut so short.

'I think it stung Anne's pride,' Damien went on in a weary, relentless tone. 'And there was Brett, only too ready to take up the slack. I didn't exactly throw her into Brett's arms, but I might as well have done for all the difference it made.'

'She had a choice, Damien. She knew Brett was married,' Natalie reminded him.

Damien reached out, his hands resting on her shoulders. 'Cause and effect, Natalie.'

'He had our child with him,' she said fiercely. 'Didn't she care about what my son would see and feel if she played Brett against you?'

She saw the blood drain completely from his face, leaving his skin sallow. 'It was my fault. If I'd had sex with her...if I'd invited her company...or even had Ryan with me while I adjusted a new harness...'

'What happened, Damien?'

He took a deep breath. 'It was agreed I'd make the first descent down the cliff. That suited me fine. I didn't want to be alone with Anne, just alone by myself.'

He paused, forcing himself to recall the exact sequence of events. 'Brett and Anne were chatting by the tent when I left them. Ryan was bouncing and catching his ball. I went to my four-wheel drive. I had ropes and harnesses in the back. I fossicked around to find what I needed, taking more time than was necessary because of the bitterness in my heart.'

His fingers dug into her flesh. 'The ball did go over the cliff, Natalie. I heard Ryan calling out for Daddy to get his ball for him. I picked up my gear, slouched out from behind the Range Rover, and saw Brett and Anne. They were embracing inside the tent. Ryan saw them. He started flailing at them with his fists and crying, ''She's not my Mummy!'''

'Oh God!' Tears spurted into Natalie's eyes.

'Then Ryan hurtled out of the tent. Brett broke away from Anne to follow him. He stumbled over a tent peg. I saw that Ryan was running blindly, straight towards the cliff edge. I yelled out to him. He took no notice. He was too upset by what he'd witnessed.

'I started running, shouting. Brett picked himself up. He was closer to Ryan than I was. He ran as fast as he could, yelling and screaming at Ryan to stop. It was a mad, frantic dash. Ryan just kept going...without looking...over the edge...and Brett...Brett dived after him as though he could catch him in mid-air and somehow bring him safely back from the fall.'

Natalie flinched away, felt her path to an armchair and collapsed into it, weeping uncontrollably. Damien crouched beside her. A pile of tissues were pressed into her hand. He hugged her shoulders tightly and drew her other hand gently against his chest.

'Please...go on,' she begged, trying ineffectually to mop up the flow of tears. 'Tell me...the rest. I want to know.'

With a heavy sigh Damien withdrew his embrace and moved away. He sat on the sofa opposite her, leaning forward, forearms resting on his knees, his eyes full of sympathy and concern as he told her what she wanted to know.

'I had my mobile phone in the Range Rover. I ran back to it and called for help. I slapped Anne out of her hysteria. My mind was working in overdrive. My thoughts only for you. I told Anne what she was to say when help came. She understood. She would be the only witness. She would only have had a fragmentary glimpse of what happened. Neither she nor Brett would be implicated in Ryan's death. There would be no scandal.

'I went down the cliff on the ropes. When I reached the bottom, I worked my way around to where their bodies lay. They were together,

Natalie. Brett's arm was flung across Ryan. There was nothing anyone could do...for either of them.'

Natalie closed her eyes. Had Brett caught their son? Had he held him...held him tight? 'He did love Ryan,' she choked out, wanting it to have been that way...having the comfort of each other before the end came. 'He was...mostly...a good father, Damien.'

'If he hadn't done what he did to you...he would have been...a good man.'

Natalie tried to stem a fresh flood of tears.

'I hadn't realised,' Damien continued, 'until that moment, how much Brett loved his son. I knew he was proud of him...as he was proud of you. I didn't know he couldn't bear losing Ryan.'

Natalie shook her head. It was more than that. In many ways she had known Brett better than Damien had. She swallowed hard several times, took a deep breath. This was the time for truth. For absolute truth. No holding back. Damien was shouldering blame and guilt that had to be shared by all of them. Herself included. She would come to that.

'There was more than his love for Ryan involved in his headlong leap over the cliff, Damien. I'm sure of it. Brett couldn't have borne knowing Ryan died because of what he'd done. He had to answer to me. It would have been the

end of everything he cared about. It *was* the end.
I think he knew that. Maybe not in any decisive
way, but intuitively.'

Damien gave her words heavy consideration,
then slowly nodded. 'Perhaps, you're right. If I
hadn't taken Anne, though——'

'If I had gone, or kept Ryan at home with
me...' Natalie cut in purposefully.

'You were sick.'

'I wasn't sick.'

Damien frowned, his eyes uncomprehending
as though he couldn't accept what she was saying.

'I pretended to be sick. Because I didn't want
to go. Because I couldn't stand going...'

'Why not? You liked camping. You liked the
mountains, the outdoor life.'

She flushed. 'You were going to be with us,
Damien. For the whole weekend. You, living in
the tent next to ours with whatever woman you
took along. Because of that, Brett would want
me. It always happened. The thought of you
making love to another woman in the next tent.
It had got to the point that I fantasised about
you when he had sex with me. I hated myself for
it. I couldn't bear to go. I made myself sick
thinking about it. I actually threw up.'

'Why did you punish yourself like that? You
had a right to say no.'

'I'm telling *you* what happened, Damien.
Please listen.'

His mouth tightened, holding his feelings in as he concentrated on her words.

'Because I was physically sick, Brett wouldn't leave Ryan with me. He said I should rest and not be worried about looking after him. Besides, Ryan might catch whatever bug I had. It was better for him to go away for the weekend with his father and Uncle Damien. Because I couldn't face admitting the truth, that you were the cause of my problem, I let Ryan go...and I stayed at home.'

'It was a reasonable decision, Natalie,' Damien said in a reassuring tone.

'It was a lie. Don't you see? We all contributed to what happened. None of us foresaw the consequences of our actions, and we all have guilt to bear. But to say that you were more at fault over Ryan's death...that simply isn't true, Damien.'

He searched her eyes with urgent intensity, wanting to believe. 'After all I've told you...you don't blame me, Natalie?' he asked in a tensely strained voice.

'Wasn't it you who put the ball back in Ryan's bag?'

'It took me hours to find it.' He made a helpless little gesture with his hands. 'Ryan loved playing with balls. It was all that was left. It was something I could do. It seemed ... important at the time. It was the last thing Ryan had ...'

His eyes blurred with tears. 'I'm sorry, Natalie. I wanted . . . I didn't know how to make it up to you. All I could do was . . . find a ball . . . and concoct a story . . . to lessen the blow.'

He bowed his head, shaking it in hopeless anguish. 'At the funeral, Anne wasn't sobbing because she had lost Brett. Like me, she was overwhelmed by what happened. She didn't want to be near me, any more than I wanted to be near her. The memory, the unforgettable memory of the consequences of our actions . . .'

'But you've been in touch since then,' Natalie said, sure in her own mind that it was no coincidence that Anne Smith had *spotted* her talent. 'You knew about my publishing contract before I told you.'

She remembered how she had been going to surprise him with what she had done by her own efforts.

'Yes, I knew,' he said heavily.

'How could you be so sure I'd go to that particular house?'

'When you asked my advice on what publishers to approach, Anne's company was head of the list. With the way we both felt, you would have got the contract regardless of what you submitted.' An ironic smile lightened the strain on his face. 'As it turned out, you are a top creative talent.'

'And you are my very good friend.' Natalie pushed herself out of the chair and went to him, falling on her knees and cupping his face in her hands, forcing him to meet her eyes. She hoped they reflected what was in her soul. 'You did your best for me, Damien. You always did. You're the best friend any woman could have. Don't you think I realise that? Appreciate it? And love you for it?'

'Natalie...' A wild hope chased the anguish away. His hands swooped to grasp her underarm and lift her with him as he surged to his feet. 'Natalie, Natalie...' It was a breath of incredulous wonderment. His arms encircled her and crushed her to him, his mouth pressing hot, urgent kisses over her hair. 'I'll do everything in my power to make you happy. Anything...'

'I want to make *you* happy, Damien.'

'You have. I am.'

'I have something to tell you.'

His mouth scorched down her neck and shoulders. 'I love you, Natalie. I love you, and only you, and always will.'

His kissing stopped. His chest heaved against her breasts. He eased his embrace to look into her eyes, anxious not to make a mistake, hopeful that he had understood correctly. 'I desire you. I long for you. I lust for you.'

'So do I, for you, Damien.'

His face lit with joy and relief. 'Everything's all right.'

Before Natalie could take another breath, he had swung her around and was lowering her on to the sofa, naked desire blazing from his eyes.

'Damien, you must listen,' she half-protested, 'or I'll never get to tell you.'

'We'll be married...soon...'

'Of course we will.'

He was opening the buttons on her blouse, caressing the soft swell of her breasts, flicking his tongue across her nipples.

'Damien Chandler, if you don't stop that...'

'You're enjoying it,' he pleaded.

'Of course I am. But I want your full attention. I want to see your eyes.'

He brought his face up close to hers. 'Will this do?'

'My instincts were right, Damien,' she assured him, excitement dancing in her voice and manner at the prospect of the future they would share together, the family they would share together. 'When we were at Merlinmist something happened.'

'I know. I know,' he said with a touch of impatience. 'I remember vividly. But this is better, Natalie. Much better...'

'Something important, Damien.'

His eyes were quizzical, searching. 'What?'

'I intended to tell you this morning.'

'Don't drag it out like this. Tell me, tell me...'

'We're going to have a baby,' she announced on a deep sigh of satisfaction.

There was a mixture of awe and wonderment in his eyes. 'A baby!'

'Our child.'

His touch gentled, became almost reverential. 'I love you, Natalie. With all my heart.'

'I love you, too, Damien. With all my heart.'

'A baby,' he said simply, as if tasting the wonder of the word.

'You're going to be a father, Damien,' Natalie said firmly.

A look of soft tenderness spread over his face. He smiled, a smile that shone with love.

'You give me the gift of life.'

'You've given it to me.'

The smile spread into a grin before he kissed her. 'I'm going to be a daddy.'

HARLEQUIN PRESENTS®

Ever felt the excitement of a dangerous desire...?

The thrill of a feverish flirtation...?

Passion is guaranteed with our new selection of sensual stories.

Indulge in...

Dangerous Liaisons
Falling in love is a risky affair!

Coming next month:

Tainted Love by Alison Fraser

Harlequin Presents #1753

Clare Anderson was a prisoner of passion, a woman with a
past...and Fen Marchand clearly didn't have a high opinion
of her! But he was father to ten-year-old Miles and badly in
need of a housekeeper...so badly in need that he agreed to
take on Clare. The physical attraction between them was
powerful—but unwanted! Clare had to keep her distance.
Fen must never know that the risks she'd taken had been for
the sake of her precious son....

Available in July wherever Harlequin books are sold.

Take 4 bestselling love stories FREE

Plus get a FREE surprise gift!

Special Limited-time Offer

Mail to Harlequin Reader Service®

3010 Walden Avenue
P.O. Box 1867
Buffalo, N.Y. 14269-1867

YES! Please send me 4 free Harlequin Presents® novels and my free surprise gift. Then send me 6 brand-new novels every month, which I will receive months before they appear in bookstores. Bill me at the low price of $2.44 each plus 25¢ delivery and applicable sales tax, if any*. That's the complete price and a savings of over 10% off the cover prices—quite a bargain! I understand that accepting the books and gift places me under no obligation ever to buy any books. I can always return a shipment and cancel at any time. Even if I never buy another book from Harlequin, the 4 free books and the surprise gift are mine to keep forever.

106 BPA ANRH

Name	(PLEASE PRINT)	
Address	Apt. No.	
City	State	Zip

This offer is limited to one order per household and not valid to present Harlequin Presents® subscribers. *Terms and prices are subject to change without notice. Sales tax applicable in N.Y.

UPRES-295

©1990 Harlequin Enterprises Limited

If you are looking for more titles by

EMMA DARCY

Don't miss these fabulous stories by one of
Harlequin's most renowned authors:

Harlequin Presents®

#11496	THE VELVET TIGER	$2.89	☐
#11519	HEART OF THE OUTBACK	$2.89	☐
#11536	AN IMPOSSIBLE DREAM	$2.89	☐
#11555	THE UPSTAIRS LOVER	$2.89	☐
#11570	NO RISKS, NO PRIZES	$2.99	☐
#11579	A VERY STYLISH AFFAIR	$2.99	☐
#11592	THE LAST GRAND PASSION	$2.99	☐
#11604	THE SHEIKH'S REVENGE	$2.99	☐
#11632	THE SHINING OF LOVE	$2.99	☐
#11659	A WEDDING TO REMEMBER	$2.99 U.S.	☐
		$3.50 CAN.	☐

(limited quantities available on certain titles)

TOTAL AMOUNT	$
POSTAGE & HANDLING	$
($1.00 for one book, 50¢ for each additional)	
APPLICABLE TAXES*	$_____
TOTAL PAYABLE	$_____
(check or money order—please do not send cash)	

To order, complete this form and send it, along with a check or money order
for the total above, payable to Harlequin Books, to: **In the U.S.:** 3010 Walden
Avenue, P.O. Box 9047, Buffalo, NY 14269-9047; **In Canada:** P.O. Box 613,
Fort Erie, Ontario, L2A 5X3.

Name: _____

Address: _____ City: _____

State/Prov.: _____ Zip/Postal Code: _____

*New York residents remit applicable sales taxes.
  Canadian residents remit applicable GST and provincial taxes.   HEDBACK1

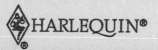
HARLEQUIN®

HARLEQUIN PRESENTS®

Don't be late for the wedding!

Be sure to make a date for the happy event—

The first in our tantalizing new selection of stories...

Wedlocked!
Bonded in matrimony, torn by desire...

Next month, watch for:
A Bride for the Taking by Sandra Marton
Harlequin Presents #1751

Dorian had a problem, and there was only one solution: she had to become Jake Prince's wife! Jake was all too willing to make love to her, but they both knew their marriage was a sham. The trouble was, Dorian soon realized she wanted more, much more, than a few nights of bliss in his arms and a pretense of love—she wanted that pretense to become reality....

Available in July wherever Harlequin books are sold.

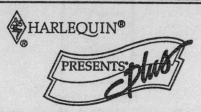

HARLEQUIN®

PRESENTS Plus

Presents Plus—the power of passion!

Coming next month:

Edge of Deception by Daphne Clair
Harlequin Presents Plus #1749

Tara's ex-husband was getting married—but, five years
after their bitter parting, it finally dawned on Tara that
she still loved him! She knew it was a hopeless love.
Their past had been shadowed by an edge of deception,
and neither could forget that he'd accused Tara of an
unforgivable sin....

and

Enemy Within by Amanda Browning
Harlequin Presents Plus #1750

Ryan Douglas was simply the wrong man for Michaela!
His reputation as a womanizer was legendary, and he
was convinced Mickey had encouraged her half sister
to run off with his wealthy nephew. Now Ryan was
determined to find the missing pair—and insisted
Michaela join him!

Harlequin Presents Plus
The best has just gotten better!

Available in July wherever Harlequin books are sold.

Announcing
the New Pages & Privileges™ Program
from Harlequin® and Silhouette®

Get All This FREE
With Just One Proof-of-Purchase!

- **FREE Travel Service** with the guaranteed lowest available airfares plus 5% cash back on every ticket

- **FREE Hotel Discounts** of up to 60% off at leading hotels in the U.S., Canada and Europe

- **FREE Petite Parfumerie** collection (a $50 Retail value)

- **FREE $25 Travel Voucher** to use on any ticket on any airline booked through our Travel Service

- **FREE Insider Tips Letter** full of fascinating information and hot sneak previews of upcoming books

- **FREE Mystery Gift** (if you enroll before June 15/95)

And there are more great gifts and benefits to come!
Enroll today and become Privileged!
(see insert for details)